# THE SHAH LEGACY: Gold Bonds, Billions, and Yellow Cake

A Dark Cave Novel

By

## Michael Plunkett

W & B Publishers

USA

For information:
W & B Publishers, LLC
9001 Ridge Hill Street
Kernersville, North Carolina 27285
www.a-argusbooks.com
ISBN:978-0-6159641-0-2
ISBN: 0-6159641-0-9


Book Cover designed by Dubya

Printed in the United States of America

## Contents:

Chapter 1

An Eventful Ride

The quickening breeze grew chilled as the clouds overhead progressed, grey and ominous. *Will I make it to the house garage in time?*

The stout motor of the Harley purred steadily, a re-bored carburetor jet .0070 over-bore, allowing the fuel to flow effortlessly to the big jugs, pounding stridently, rhythematicaly, in a roaring, oscillating cadence, the bike in the highest gear.

I had been in a downpour before, you know, the kind you can't see through, unleashed in a moment of time, from zero to deluge in three seconds. The roads would be flooded, the road gutters swollen with a small river of run off to navigate through without losing traction, hydro-planning or slipping into a curve.

At age 67 I reflected upon whether I was too old for such an adventure as was imminent below my handlebars. These were not the days of the three-piece suits, Raphael, Lanvin, or Halsuade; the ride, a Lear Jet above these clouds by 20,000 feet, cocktail in hand and $20,000 spending money in my briefcase. There were a lot of places to "Duck in" under those former circumstances, but not now. Just me, the clouds and the road. Days past are truly past. No tattoo's—but I was an "Easy Rider" these days.

Of course, all the advertisements and the genre philosophy professed that I was Free, Free... and I must admit that the wind through my hair was addictive, the landscape before and all around me a special treat. There was a certain sense of commanding your situation and destiny, moment by moment, as you had to interact with traffic synergistically and sometimes instantaneously, in life or death exchanges. *White knuckles, grinning, white and tight! What a rush!*

*Or is this the act of an adult/child, who needs unbridled stimulus without the responsibilities of mundane living?* Dramatizing, rationalizing, and legitimatizing this errant behavior. *Ohg! Go away, logic; had enough of that.* I built a fine and successful business, only to have trusted colleagues conspire to undo its structure and future. Sometimes spitefully.

I was not naive of human nature and greed, but yes, too trusting of loyalty and friendship. If you fail to mind your business, it will surely mind you. The higher up that flagpole you get, the more bare ass you leave exposed for those who would shoot at it and shoot they will! If you fail to stay up there and slide down, sometimes you are too old to re-start or re-coup.

So let's find another challenge, like keeping your ass alive on two wheels at 70 MPH! *Whew! High Ho Silver! Away! Beats clearing the check-out lines at Wal-Mart with your "Border Patrol" cap, scrambled eggs and all, for kicks.* Not quite the America I grew up in. Actually there weren't any Wal Marts back then in my part of the country. Old Wally did a heck of a job!

Actually, as I honestly reflect, the Mexican people who populate Wal-Marts in my area have made a very good impression. They are industrious, hard working, helpful individuals with real family values, for the most part. Yeah, in a pinch, you can count on `em.

But immigration should be controlled. We are overrun by hordes of illegal immigrants, as was Rome before its fall. Proposed laws favor these in-terlopers as a voter base. Food stamps in one hand and a voter registration form in the other. Not to mention 99 weeks of unemployment benefits.

*So much change,* I allowed my mind to contin-ue wandering, *American history is not taught well anymore in our schools.*

We elected a "mixed-race candidate" with a

1953 "Buick Grill" for a smile as President, who seems to be in way over his head in matters of state and foreign policy. He—P.O.T.U.S—injects his personality into local news issues but only when it concerns his personal agenda for enhancement of his racial comrades. He acts out in way to puerile for his office. Presidents should avoid such polarizing, local issues and remain above involvement on this level.

A 'reformer', he sponsors and favors socialistic polices, rather than American "exceptionality." In his own life this President had benefited much from government minority, entitlement programs. Notably aid for foreign students. His past is a little sketchy and any school records or transcripts have been blocked from decimation.

He had managed to get to Harvard without the where-with-all to do so. His family was, at best, lower middle-class in status. It is assumed that he benefited from a foreign exchange scholarship program but would have to have had another citizenship status at that time. All of this background was shrouded in secrecy. Most of his classmates have no recollection of him, even those in the same curriculum. Strange since he was purported to be involved in the Harvard Law Review. It sounded to many like a contrived pedigree for political enhancement. His handler had a reputation for this type of grooming in the state Legislature.

For an "Educated" guy, he lacks originality, always speaking from a script with the aid of a teleprompter. Funny, if there is a malfunction technically with the screen, he becomes obviously flustered, even reading the same sentence twice. He admits to being lazy and doing a lot of drugs in school. The "Powers that be" have a malleable puppet who smiles orates and dances!

We have had a resurgence of the 1970's Black Panthers presence, clubs in hand, and a Para-Military, Mau Mau demeanor, intimidating arrivals at the voting booth. Our Attorney General does nothing, despite the obvious infraction of our voting laws. Another, the AG is another "mixed" guy! Even the intuitional AARP has dropped its A's and just politically P's on its constituents.

Now, I am not accustomed to using euphemisms when it comes to describing one of the many races on our planet We have a Black Caucus in Congress, an NAACP—'C' for colored—and any number of other racial organizations but we have gone from saying Negro to Colored to Black to African American for people who have never been to Africa in a frantic attempt to keep from indicating the color of their skin. I am expecting Congress to outlaw mirrors because a black person might walk in front of one, accidentally, and discover his blackness! We must be "Politically Correct."

That old 'N' word which rates right up there

with Blaspheming God these days—which I can't write here because an editor would have an anal crunch—to me describes not a person's color but a behavior pattern. It can be used pejoratively or very friendly. And once in the vernacular, it should be alright for anybody to use, in a respectful way. A recent jury ruled out using it at all, even black on black.

These people should be proud of their race. There have been so many accomplishments in science, music, sports, and in education excellence by their people. They have risen to the pinnacle of government, courts and the arts. Some have become Billionaires. Many are corporate CEO's and as advanced as any other race in this country.

This status was hard won but it was won. Of course, excuses, rationalizations are always easier than the hard work it takes for anyone to rise to prominence. Least important should be the color of a person's skin. The concept of "Political Correctness" only perpetuates the employment of prejudice. Mutual respect for character should control and prevail in social exchange. The purr of the Harley motor encouraged my personal, mental essay.

The I.R.S. has conjured up new fines and the addition of thousands of personnel to manage, of all things, our health care. Who would have thought that this originally volunteer tax institution would have morphed into policing our health care?

Critically thinking, gray mass would have seen this onerous development, coming. An outworking of "Power Corrupts." Finish, Ay, mate ? The way to justify your Government job efficacy is to just say No! Now we will have to work it out.

My musing was now wandering into nostalgia,....

Oh, the '90's! I was involved in private placement banking round the world. From Morin County, California to the Sheiks of the Middle East. Millions were invested. I would Fax a contract before breakfast and Truanch before noon. "Swift" wire transfers, $100,000 minimum was the entry level. My mind movie projected on; Swiss Bankers, Dr. Schwitz, dealing through the back door of the bank, proffering 11 Billion worth of German Gold-Backed Bearer Bonds,( Art Objects, such as; "Clark's, Daws, Rheinolbe Union's, these bonds backed in gold by J.P. Morgan Bank, pre world war II.)

There was much intrigue—the Deutsche Bundes Bank, in Germany, wanting to decay serial numbers of the debt instruments, to avoid having to redeem them.

The arrangement was that they were usually "blocked up" against an 80% loan, to then, enter into a $500 Million, Federal Roll Program. The resulting 7 ½ X 10's, series notes, issued by Top 100

Western European Banks (over 200 Billion in assets, now a Trillion) were re- sold at a discount in 500 Million Blocks around the world to investors.

They were called "7 ½ by 10's." 7 1/2 % interest, by 10 year, series notes. Also, sold off to the Hong Kong, Banks, etc., Heady days ! An exciting, adrenalin packed, game. I had the original, big foot-long, cell phone glued to my ear and faxed contracts, around the world, at all hours—time zones mandating work times.

Peruvian Gold Bonds. Watch out! You could be shot dead departing the plane if it were known that you had one in your briefcase, rather than have the national bank redeem them at current value. A billion per, or more. Adding to the overall intrigue. It was a rush with the promise of huge commissions in the offing. Had many a "Jack Denials," (sic) to sort this all out at the end of a day. The great elixir. That oil of conversation. My bright red Jag, turning heads. Heady days, indeed! The so-called facilitator is still running the streets of London as far as I know.

When a "Program" opened, there would be a frenzied effort to "get in." Reminiscent of the floor of the stock exchange. Investors and their attorneys throwing money at you, 400K, 600K; a mid eastern deep voice, broken English, "I can get you 20 million." "Hurry, the program will fill-up and close." "These are USD and sponsored by the Federal Reserve Bank." Although the Federally sponsored programs were legitimate, I then found that much the industry was pretty much a scam. There was a thread of truth which kept you going but I had ruined a family by then—mine.

Now these days, the excitement came from Zoom, Zoom, throttle twisting, torqueing through traffic. White knuckles and imminent death pending. *Whattya'h goanna do ?* Something about that strident sound. Compressed Co2 escaping through the exhaust pipes. *Oh, not just any pipes. Screaming Eagle pipes. Is my hair on fire yet? Did age dummy me down to this level of excitement? Even grew a white beard. What a picture!*

In my younger days, I used to own and fly a Navion. Built by Ryan Aviation and later, North American Rockwell, they were used as reconnaissance planes for the Navy. A high performance mono-wing aircraft with a retractable landing gear and a variable pitch prop and cow flaps. It was a slide canopy, four-seater, called the "Truck of the sky." You had to climb up on the wing and slide the canopy back to get in. No doors.

The camber on the wing made it very stable. You could fly at flap speed and go into a 60 degree turn and look straight down the wing at almost 90 degrees to the ground. It was also useful for flying between Condo towers at the beach. *What the hell, they were there!* The FAA wasn't pleased. *Nosy damn residents!*

Used to storm Mom and the kids in her new Caddy... convertible, (birthday present) top down, coming home from Gettysburg, PA. Ye Ha! I was making 10 Grand a month in the late 60's, early '70s.

We had an air strip at the resort we lived in. A buddy and only partner was making a straight-in approach, so he didn't go through the landing pattern and consequently, the landing check list. I had been on him about hot landings, as it was hard on landing the gear. Potential maintenance nightmare. "This isn't an aircraft carrier here. It's a 3,500 foot paved runway with very little room for error. Mountains surrounding. Plan your approach and just set the plane down quietly, just before a stall and you will meet the runway with smooth chirps from the wheels."

He lined up the straight-in approach, throttling back , wings level , falling to a stall just above the runway. Big smile, this is smooth, smooth, he reflected, Right up until the prop started to chew up the runway! He had forgotten to drop the landing gear! So much for circumventing the checklist! Shock through the prop cracked the crankshaft on the Lycoming 260 B and that was the end of our

"Snoopy."

Enough of this self adulating, reminiscing. A pick-up truck full of low-information folks was running up on my motorcycle rear fender, way too close, as Yey-hoo's (country boys) often do for kicks, trying to intimidate the cyclist. I could see the two in front seat in my side-view mirror, talking and laughing at one another, urging each other on. I applied light pressure to my brake, flashing the LED taillight; it shown brightly, flashed sequentially. The road was moist from the earlier local shower, leaving an occasional slippery spot where car engine oil had leaked on the pavement surface. I knew if I had to make a sudden stop, the pick-up would likely run over me.

White knuckles, now. I was stiffing with fear, not agile. *Damn, I don't like this! What's wrong with those guys?*

*Whoa!* A small gasoline tanker truck suddenly pulled out from a side street, I could see the driver on her cell phone - oblivious to what was about to happen until the last second. Was I in a dwarf brain time warp?

I dropped a gear and twisted the throttle in an attempt to accelerate around her. This was my only hope; teeth gritting, eyes squinting, relying on muscle memory to guide me through the maneuver. Anticipating the inevitable bone-breaking crash. Didn't think I'd make it. And then, with maybe 2 inches to spare, I cleared the front fender, as she slammed on the brakes of her 10 ton vehicle.

I think she must have dropped her caller!

Because of the sharp maneuver I had to make, the geometry of the tracking front wheel to the back was devastatingly warped and I had to wrestle control of the front wheel trajectory! I shifted my body weight in a panic, hoping for control of my slipping, sliding missile. The laws of physics in motion became distorted, unfriendly, unbalanced to wrestle with. *Shifting weight to compensate.*

*Oh my Lord! I am heading for the draining ditch along the side of the road. Long grass, mud and water. Can I avoid it ? Or give in to the slide down crash !* Adrenalin rush! *I don't want to feel the pain.* Here I am, a "White Beard," heading toward 70 years, about to break some extremity, or worse, wondering in an instant of extreme and cogent clarity, *What the hell I was doing out on this Harley Sportster, at my age?* Brittle bones, an eternity to heal, went through my mind in a flash. *Well here it comes! I can't save it! Oh Shit!*

In that instant—the things you notice with eye splitting clarity. The muddy water coming up fast, *How deep?* And a small squirrel running like hell to save himself from this hunk of metal falling from the sky.

I had a Helmut on and ultimately just resigned myself and hoped for the best with a lighting fast but intense prayer. Don't know if it was heard as it was perforated with curse words.

The front wheel was the first to break traction with the road and slide, descending down the bank into the muck. There was a fence up on the other side separating the road from the grazing acreage. Can you imagine? I am thinking, *"Are there any Bulls up there?"* during my flight downward. Then followed the back wheel sliding out from under the rigid frame of the bike. Well, it only follows that with motorcycles, where the front wheel goes, the back is sure to follow.

Before I was impacted by the chocolate-colored slush, I heard, all at once in a split second, hardly a time you could measure, and as loud as a Howitzer cannon, a thunderous, ear-splitting; a rush of hot, displaced air rolled over me in the ditch. I felt intense heat, a wall of it, *This can't be me!*

Accompanying this was the sound of metal crunching, tires squealing, horns blowing, people screaming, unintelligibly.

With a gooey splash, I came to an abrupt but somewhat soft rest. I felt a stabbing pain in my left leg. I landed in an explosion of water and mud. The last thing I saw was a discarded beer can. My nose bashed into it. *Was my head bleeding? You know how those head wounds bleed,* I thought.

But what was that I heard? It was behind me, I sensed. I had to disentangle myself from my 590 pound skewed handlebars and get up the muddy bank to see what was up. People were running everywhere but only a few towards me. Maybe 10-12 were running behind me. My eyes followed and with shock and a pain in my lungs, I saw a spectacle like none I had ever experienced or felt.

There was blistering heat, a tower of flame and black smoke masking its origin. In glimpses through it, I could see a carbon burnt cylinder with a large hole in its side and a scorched pick-up truck partially inside the hole. In a split second, it came to me. This was the top and left side of the tanker truck that I had to scramble to avoid hitting and why I was situated in the ditch. A moment of confusion ensued as my mind sought some form of a logic block that would explain this image.

Thinking now, *Those Yea-hoo's that were following so close on my rear, pointing and laughing, obliviously didn't make it around that driver on the cell phone who was running the stop sign.* Black smoke and the smell of rubber burning and there it was; front grill and windshield partially inserted in the hole but pointed to the sky. I saw the truck through the flames. There was—*wait a mi-*

*nute! Is that a face held fast by a broken wind-shield?* There was blood boiling over the hood. And suddenly the stench of flesh burning. I was screaming! "Oh my God. I can't believe this! This is not my fault. This is not my fault! Not!" I continued to screamed, inwardly.

Then a man came close to me asking if I was all right. "I saw the whole thing. Used to ride myself, as a young guy." (I reflected again on my age) *No, this was not my fault*, I reassured my ego, thanking God I was alive. I couldn't imagine that the other three were alive. I knew one wasn't.

I did not want to walk around to the other side of the tanker truck, the point of impact, afraid of what carnage I would find. Who wants those memories? I heard the distant cycle of sirens wailing. OK—in addition to the growing crowd of onlookers, people were assisting, although no one was able to get close. The heat was just intense. "Medical help is on the way," I told myself.

I knew there would be questions. On the spot investigations. I looked for the guy who said he witnessed the whole thing, franticly. I might well need his assistance with the cops. I wanted this to end today. There he was! Gesticulating wildly to another couple, seemingly pleased and excited as though he witnessed a 100 yard run back from his spot on the 50 yard line at the home team game.

That he had such a front seat to this catastrophic cacophony. Here come the Medics on arriving on the scene.

"Ah Sir, Sir," I limped and wobbled favoring my left leg, throbbing now, over near to him. "Sir, did you say you saw this whole thing?"

"Oh yeah, from start to this! Terrible, Terrible. Those three are all dead. Are you alright, sir?" he asked me. "You know you've got a small cut on the bridge of your nose and your brow where your helmet came down on your forehead."

"Oh, I didn't know, can't feel it."

"You better have them check you out," he intoned. "You had a bad fall down into that ditch."

"Yeah," I said, "good thing it was full of grass and water. Will you help me tell the cops what happened, 'course I didn't see what happened to them, they were behind me and I was in the ditch by then."

"Yes, I know. Told ya, I saw the whole thing. Don't know how you missed the front of that truck. I think the bumper might have grazed you, putting you off the road."

"I know it was close," I said.

He raised his arm and beckoned a nearby paramedic to come over, telling me I ought to sit down. They didn't even know about me in any capacity related to the accident.

Finally the word, through other witnesses,

came to the Fireman Paramedics that a motorcycle was also involved on the other side of the burning carcass of the fuel truck. One football-sized guy with a fireman's hat rounded the corner around the front of the fuel truck and beheld my crippled white steed, low in the trough of water. I was standing with my witness close at hand, bleeding a little. "Sir, were you involved in this incident here," as he swept his arm widely to include the caustic panorama of belching black smoke, flashing lights and sirens and HASMAT vehicles still approaching.

"I was in front of it, sir. The ones in the pick-up truck were riding my ass. Thought it was funny until the truck pulled out. I was hair, teeth and eyeballs, trying to avoid hitting the truck. Barely got around it. Actually might have grazed my leg and put me into that catawampus slide that put me into that ditch over there. Guess they couldn't stop in time"

Looking now at my cut nose and forehead, he said, "I am Jack Williams, Paramedic with the Delano County Fire Department.

Another assistant had rushed up to us with a chair. "Think you ought to sit down here while I assess you injuries. Where exactly does it hurt?" He gently rubbed my shoulder to see if I winced in pain. "Do you feel any pain here," He said, in a quiet, reassuring voice.

"No," I said, "just my left leg, but not too bad,

think I just bruised my knee."

Jack rolled his fingers over the area to judge the intensity of my reaction. I jerked. "Whoa", he said. "Ought to get that X Rayed, We can transport you to Community Hospital right now. Those others are all dead and I have three ambulances here waiting. They will need the coroners' wagon."

"Alright, whatever you say, sir."

He got my name and age. Observing my bloodied white beard, he said, "Not for nothing, Mike, but aren't you getting a little old for this hobby?"

"Live to ride and Ride to live", I repeated the Harley Davidson slogan with a slight smile."

"Yeah, Right" he scoffed. "You came damn close to being back there," he pointed to the scene to his right. He waved the ambulance unit up to where we were and then turned to my witness, asking, "You see this, sir?"

A floodgate of monolog ensued in an exited voice, arms gesticulating, a crescendo voicing higher and ever higher, feeding on its own thought fuel, describing, in minute detail, the progression of events culminating in this sad conflagration. "A real shame, you know. This guy," pointing to me, "is lucky as hell he wasn't a second earlier or you wouldn't be able to find him in that tangled mess."

Chapter 2

*A trip to the Hospital,*
*An Old Acquaintance Found,*
*Let's Explore The Possibilities,*
*How many Bonds, Did You Say?*

I was helped onto a stretcher, which literally popped out of the back of the medical unit, and before I knew it, I was alone with an assistant, who was masking me with oxygen, starting an IV. I heard the door slam behind me. He took my blood pressure and immediately reported all on a small lap top. Asking if I was allergic to any medicines.

Then it hit me. "Hey what about my bike?" I yelled.

"They'll take it in to county impound," he replied.

"County what,?" I said. "That'll cost money!" And his answer was masked by the sound of our siren and the roll of the diesel motor of the unit, accelerating away.

"Do you have an ID and insurance card, sir?" The hospital intake nurse ran alongside my gurney as we entered the deep-walled elevator. I remembered wondering why she was using a bejeweled pen. God I hope she wasn't paid on commission! And I knew I had been irrevocably captured in the Insuro/Hospito complex and would not be released until the very last test of a cavalcade of possible Ism's and Ology's had milked my insurance for the benefit of the hospital's spread sheet debits for indigents. Let's balance the books on this guy! Test his heart, brain and scrotum for signs of ology's and Isim's. Report on this Medicare/Medicaid form. Medicaid ! We've struck it rich! Hey, this will cover 6-10 indigent accounts. Use the blue coded strips for Mary, the bookkeeper downstairs. I imagined the scenario in my super cynical prospective.

There was an old lady in the second car behind the pick-up who had narrowly avoided the collision but peed her pants and had a heart attack. I could hear her thanking God and wailing for her husband, in the same breath. They took her out of the car in three pieces. Her artificial leg, her torso and her false teeth, hitting the dashboard! Even so, she was fine.

Oh, those sounds and smells of a hospital. How had I forgotten? It was only a bruised knee.

Oh, the ether odor in the hallways was caustic! *Thought they stopped using that stuff.*

A nurse, RN, cute, about 40, bent over my face and asked if I knew my name and why I was here.

"My name is Julius Slick from Pumpkin Crick; My brother is Sam Katz, suits and hats; My uncle is Sid Swartz, suits and shorts. I sell Toaster's, Roaster's Hair Dryers and Chicken Fryers, all kinds of cooking utensils and I am here to get out of housework!" I joked. I love to be contrary. You can say anything if you have a smile on your face.

"What's that smell, Nurse?" Do you still use ether here?

"No, sir," came her terse reply. Then, "Hey, Jane; bring me a needle, we have a lively one here." she exclaimed to the nurse out in the hall. My smile disappeared, fast!

"Hey, do you guys mark your extremities with permanent marker before amputations at this facility?" I tried again to break the ice. "I read where City General cut the wrong foot off a patient the other day and I am here to be circumcised!" I joked.

"Oh, do you have two of those?" she countered

"Well, sometimes it feels like it," I said. I was reaching, trying to stay in the kibitz, sparing. Nervous, I guess.

"Watch out , we can fix that too," Mr. Slick."

Well, you only need one, if you read the instructions!" I quipped.

There was a lull in the conversation. "Can I order a Jack Daniels now? My mom used to say, "It was 5 o' clock somewhere."

"I'll see what I can do", she replied crisply as she left my room, without looking back.

I attempted to settle in and turned on the overhead TV. There was the news and what do you suppose? There I was! In living color, and the flaming truck and the emergency vehicles. God, what mayhem from the Helicopter exposure.

I wanted to call somebody and lament how I was the guy over in the corner of the shot with Jack, the Paramedic. Woe is me, woe is me. Who... Who would be the most sympatric? "Hello, Hey Trish, are you watching channel 7 news? ....."

In pops a head. *Think I recognize him. Nah, been years.* Then a double take. Head pops in again. "Bobby," I yelled. "Bobby King!" This was an American nickname or alias for Buruse Backka, grand nephew of The Shah of Iran. There were many nephews. We were old friends and business associates. The Shah had been deceased now some years. Bobby was a good-looking, big-smile guy from the past.

"Is that you, Mike? I was looking for my sister's room and what are you doing in here?"

I pointed up to the TV. He looked puzzled. "That's me, in the lower left hand corner. You can barely make out my bike handle bars down in that ditch." I recounted the story to wide eyes and an O shaped mouth

"No shit? Really?! Are you kidding me? Man!" Then the million dollar smile, pristine white, looked like it was back-lit, it glowed. "Are you all right now?" That was Bobby King. We had had some good times together 20 years ago. He had aged into a handsome, Middle-Eastern distinguished gentleman.

"I lost track of you when you left from Virginia after that real estate deal to go to California."

"Wow! That was a long time ago," he opined.

"Yeah, what happened out there?" I inquired. "Do you have kids? Married?"

"One daughter, now 32."

"I'll bet she's a beauty, got a picture?" I said.

"I got into some Real Estate at first and then a stock broker," he said in accented English. "Whatted' you do?"

"Actually, I went into some *Private Placement Banking* after leaving DEL Marketing. It was sold," I replied, trying to make the banking sound very important and exotic.

"What?" he said.

"Oh, you know—Federal Roll Programs," I said, with a flip of my hand.

"Never heard of that", he said.

"It gets a little complicated," I said. "Hey, I

dealt with a couple of your guys over there in the middle east. Sheik somebody, I can't remember right now."

His eyebrows rose with inquiry. "Really? No kidding?" his interest piqued.

"Yeah, I was blocking German-Gold backed-bearer bonds, issued pre-war 1922 - 1930, each worth today monetized at about 1-5 M, blocked-up as a credit facility, for investment into a Federal Roll Programs. Lots of money involved."

I was looking for a little relief now. I said, "Hey, man, I don't want to keep you from your sister, better go and see her now. Come back. It's great to see you man. I'll tell you about it later. Got real exiting, right up until the FBI got involved."

Last time we were together, I was the National sales director and Executive Vice President of D.E.L. Marketing. We ran seven projects, some writing $1 M a week in individual sales contracts. I had been a project director of one or two of them— we had seven in the Northeast—and was responsible for this level of success at two of them. In addition, I had 580 Sales people to manage, train and motivate, so I was well known through the company. I was known to earn between $3,500 and up to $20,000 dollars a week back in the 70's and I was fun to be around. Easy come, easy go. I could Spend it! And I was a generous sort of guy. So my history was known to Bobby.

I had just allowed my head to rest against my pillow for a while and oh! The knee was throbbing. "Nurse," I pushed the call button.

"May I help you sir?"

"Could I have something for my pain?"

"We can bring an Aspirin, Sir."

"No kidding. An aspirin?. Can you do a little better than that?"

"Not until after you get back from X-Ray, sir."

"OK," I said with resignation, and I dropped my head back on my pillow.

I had barely closed my eyes when in walked the Sheriff and two of his deputies. They noticed that I had the TV on to the news channel. "Did you know those two in the truck?" as he peered close at my name tag.

"No, sir," I replied," but they were sure on my butt. Following way too close. Intimidating. Seem to think it was a joke."

"Yes sir, they have done this before, he said. "These were the Johnson boys, from Prince William County, right next door. They have come here before with their shenanigans. Caused a motorcycle accident last time. Hurt the guy pretty bad. They got a police record for that.

"Yes sir. I got out of their way just in time,

when that truck pulled out. Hey, that girl was looking down at her cell phone. Texting maybe," I offered.

"Yes sir. Is that the way it was?" He was writing. "We found a phone but couldn't read the screen. Too burnt. More or less melted, you know."

"Oh," I replied, thinking of those last seconds before the blast of heat and fire rolled over me down in the ditch. Whew! It made me shiver.

Oh, here was the desk nurse with my Aspirin.

"How strong is that medicine, Mame? We are not finished here yet. Will he go to sleep?"

"Oh, I don't think so, Sherriff. It's just an aspirin."

"He's lucky that's all he needs. See that mess?" He pointed to the TV. Now a big crane was moving into place, trying to get a hook on the top of the tanker. There was a steel islet welded there. They could lift and pull the tanker upright from there. Big as a whale, the black, soot-covered, irregular-shaped, blown-out cylinder rolled over up-right with a mighty bounce reaction due to the inertia it had developed. You could hear glass breaking and settling, even over the TV speakers. Boy, was I thankful to be away from that scene.

The Sheriff, the deputies and myself all

watched silently while the scene unfolded before us on the TV. A huge flatbed had pulled into the camera's view, presumably to haul the remains away and out of the intersection.

"Well, really, sir, that's all we need for now. One of these deputies will stop by before you are discharged with a final report for you to sign."

I nodded my head affirmatively, just wanting them to leave.

"Do you know when that will be? he asked.

"No, Sir," I said, "but maybe tomorrow, since they have to X-Ray my knee yet." It was getting late in the afternoon and I assumed it would be dragged out until tomorrow.

"Ok. Oh, we towed your bike to our impound lot. Didn't look too bad to me. You can pick it up anytime. No charge for up to 3 days under these circumstances, Mr. Charles.

Bobby returned after checking in with his sister. "Hey, man!" Looking back up at the news coverage, he said "Man, you're lucky!"

"Yeah, always did have that horse shoe in my back pocket," I smiled. "Whattsup?" How is your sister doing and why is she here?"

"Oh, female stuff. At her age, routine, no problem."

He pulled up a chair in the room and drew

close to my bed. "You know those Gold Bonds you used to deal in, back in the 90's?"

"Yeah," I said. "Had 11 Billion committed from owners and collectors, all over the U.S. and Canada. I believe it was about that much.

"You're not going to believe this, but when I finally got back into Iran after some years, I opened an old safety deposit box in my uncle's bank and I found five stacks of them dating back to pre world war II. Are they still worth anything?" he said.

"I don't know for sure, were they issues from 1924 to 1930? There was a lawsuit in 1953, I vaguely remembered. Potentially 5M, each, monetized," I said. "If a precedent were set in Federal Court it could mean billions in obligations! Germany would like to decay them and are hungry for serial numbers. There could eventually be a U.S. taxpayer obligation, in the billions for those guaranteed by J.P. Morgan if monetized. I dropped out when the FBI stepped in and commandeered the file cabinets in my office."

Oh, was I getting 'itchy' and interested!

"Their real value these days are as art objects on top of their escalated gold appreciation value was stimulating."

"I could look into it for you, but keep it quiet , for now," I said.

"Oh yeah, man," with a big, white smile and eyes like saucers. "You know me. Seven Camel's couldn't, ..." and he trailed off, as the nurse came over again.

"There could be some danger and risk, Ol' boy," I continued. "If word got out, it could attract some strange and very serious hombres, and an alphabet of US government agencies, if you know what I mean."

"OK, My man!......., How can we get to them, remove them out of the country, through customs, etc, without arousing any attention? We'd have to take them to an off-shore banking location to avoid any taxes, but make no mistake, there would be "Fees" to pay for "Services". If the Bonds are used for "Blocking" into a credit facility in order to produce cash, what would it be used for? You already have every fire arm known to man,

Bobby," I joked. "Want a Battle ship?"

"I can get us in "diplomatically, from the old days. There is a mutual respect at a distance, if you know what I mean," he went on, with a wistful, far-away look.

As a young boy, he was privy to so many "insider" plots and intrigue that family adults didn't think he was capable of understanding.

"Couldn't stay long, though. Just get the bonds from the box and make like Mohamed and fly away."

"Yeah," I opined, "But look how many followers he had trailing along."

"And all with long, curved, knives," he quipped.

"We would need a very accommodating Depository. A numbered account. Maximum secrecy, You know, you've got to pay for those things, " I added.

"I'll leave that to you," he said. "I was looking to yield several hundred million in loan proceeds from the 'Blocking', if possible."

"What would you do with that kind of money?" I said. Thinking of a huge commission.

"I don't want to be specific right now, but I have a way through the back door of supplying capital - for scientific advancement, to the current regime for a 'Big Time' compensation arrangement. I'll split it with you! We can 'lay on the beach' anywhere in the world."

"Whoa! I exclaimed, "In Iran? What are you into, Bobby ? Scientific advancement ? Sounds like a euphemism for nuclear centrifuge technology or hardware. You know that Amah Dada Du-min a jad," I slurred, "is a crazy little dude with a Napoleon, small-man, complex."

"He's not in control", Bobby replied.

"Oh great, it's worse than that," I said. "Some turban-wrapped Ayatollah ideologue dreaming of 17 vestal virgins as consorts. Got to be crazy on the face of it! Seventeen women, running around, trying to control your ass. Oh yea, that's worth dying for! Hey, where did your people go wrong ? Too much time in hot desert tents with two-humped camels passing gas outside?" I asked, with a Brooklyn flair and gesticulation, right hand in the air.

"Let me ask you something....? Trying to understand. The Nuclear Conundrum, to me is..."

"Why would a developing country, that is, a technologically developing country want to spend billions of dollars of resources to learn to split this "Atom" for the purpose of warfare with an already, far advanced, master of the technology ? What insanity is this."

"The developed country is, in fact, trying to reduce it's already 'overkill' stockpile. So, why, whether through alliances, cooperation, or direct retaliation, and then through corresponding, opposing, alliances encourage a retaliatory, conflagration of unstoppable fire, poison air, infrastructure destruction, death, massive disease and pretty much world-wide crop failure, just to prove It has a bigger phallus! (Male orientation). Only a Human is capable of this kind of BLIND logic and self destructive thinking!"

"Oh! You want heat you say? You'll get heat all right! Where is Tom Cruise when you need him?"

"I like Harrison Ford, he countered. With him you might get Sean Connery, too."

"Go to Hell," I said.

I had just watched a high adventure movie and had a picture in my head of myself, in fatigues with an AR- 15 in tow. Oh Geeze, I banished the picture and thought, *Kid's stuff!*

"Look, we can fruitfully develop and utilize this power under agreed auspices of control, responsible to an international body. And, even get assistance and financial aid from other developed countries interested in the eleemosynary benefits for all the people."

"We want you to live and prosper," Spock would say. "Ya' just can't be that stupid with God's gifts of knowledge, through Science! And go around threatening Sovereign nations with extinction. Especially ones that can kick your ass!" I said.

"I don't know, man," I went on with my diatribe, "You're gonna' end up with the CIA, NSA, FBI, The Mossad, the Sec. State.

"Oh God! Hillary," he withered, "The Ruskies, who knows who else, in the mix. Got a bullet proof vest?"

"How trustworthy is your contact?" I asked, showing some trace of possible commitment to this intrigue. He knew from our past association in the late 70's that I, like him, was a little crazy. 'You ain't liv'in' unless your near dying', would characterize it accurately.

"You know, we're a little too old for this shit, Bobby," I queried.

A big, fluorescent smile only Bobby could do well. "C'mon man, it is de piece of cake. I'll show you that part of the world!"

"This kind of thing is what drove me to just ride my bike," I replied/ "It's the Doc Sam Sheppard syndrome."

*Well, it could be a big hit,* I mused. *Wife left 15 years, now, kids grown. Chance to leave them a big dollar legacy to squander. Hero again.?* This was growing progressively, attractive as I allowed my imagination to reach Panavision!

An orderly came in to the room with a wheel-chair. "Ready to go down to X ray?" he said cheer-fully!

I looked at Bobby and said, "I'll give this some thought, make some calls and get back with you. Can you leave your current contact info on the little pad in that drawer?" Here is a card of mine." I re-trieved one from my bedside table top where a pile of identification had been dumped when I changed into my hospital gown.

"Lots of permeations here to consider. Sounds like it has real possibilities. Last time I was in-volved in one of these transactions, I ended up in the big, red brick building in Sarasota, Florida."

He looked puzzled, so I quickly added, "The FBI building," glancing up at the orderly to see if he was listening.

"Sure, let's go," I said to the orderly. "I need to get out of here today, if I can."

It was a short trip down to the ice cold, metal, X-Ray table. Bending, pulling, twisting, manipulating and rearranging my leg for a favorable X ray shot was painful. I was beginning to wonder if I hadn't actually fractured something. Originally, I thought it was just a bad sprain. My shoulder was hurting now after X Ray tech, Gyro Jane, a big strong, no non-sense nurse, had worked her "Magic Pretzel" move on me on the cold table.

"Gee, do you do this for everybody?" I quipped.

"Only the ones that still have arms and legs," she shot back. "You are lucky." And then added, "I saw the TV this morning."

"Yes, maim," I said sheepishly. She had my leg and knee firmly in her grip.

"OK, hold still," as she disappeared behind a window in the wall. *Click*. "Ok, good". "That's it, Lucky! I will have it read by this afternoon."

I was glad to have it over with. An orderly came in and helped Gyro Jane put me into a wheelchair and back to my room we rolled. He was a nice looking young, black man.

Always interested in youthful career dreams, I asked him if he was going to pursue a medical career. Remember, I am 67 years old and have a white beard. Like a grandfather's interest, not nosey.

"Yes sir", came the reply from behind me. "I am enlisting in the US Navy and hope to get my training there."

Good for you," I said.

"Yeah, I already have my Bachelor's degree in Chemistry. They have agreed to send me to med school in the fall."

"Good people, those Navy guys", I offered. My dad was a pharmacist mate in the Coast Guard during the war. Close to the Solomon Islands, off the East coast; there were lots of German subs, just off shore, sinking our supply ships going to England, early on. He was considered the local Doc in those remote areas. He developed a private formula for sun tan lotion."

"Wow," the young man exclaimed. "Bet those were hairy times!"

"Actually, there was some secrecy and intrigue," thinking of a funny story.

"How's that, sir"?

With a chuckle, I said, "Well, when the crew needed to go on leave for a weekend in some island town, Dad was known to conveniently lose the Captain's shot record and to attempt to enforce another round of painful injections. The Captain, an old salt, would inveigh, 'How about a weekend leave to find them there records?' Yes sir, I am almost sure they are mixed up with my big stack in the medicine requisition file," Dad would say.

"As the ruse was comprehended, the young man laughed and said, "Yeah, I got it!"

We were at my door. "Hey, by the way, can I make international calls from my room"?

"Is your credit card on file"?

"Don't think so, but I can give it to you". Then I caught myself. That would be traceable. Better to buy a throw away cell phone to call my contact in Switzerland and the Turk and Cacaos Islands offshore. "Actually, never mind right now, son. Best of luck in the Navy. Anchors Away!" I stuck my thumb in the air.

Here came lunch. A short, stout, black CAN slid her cart into the room. "Whoo hooo! Are you alright? Ain't you the old man on the TeeVee this mornin? We's watching down in the laundry. You are some lucky! Shore nough blow'ed that gas truck up."

"Well no, I had just passed it when the guys behind hit it."

"Why dat driver pull out like that?, Like no one was there"?

Hands spread wide apart, "I think I saw her phone in her hand, approaching the stop sign. I had to whip around her. That's why I am in here. Went into the ditch on the other side, trying to recover my caddywhampus motorcycle."

"Hey, Whattya got for lunch," as I uncovered the thermal dome on top of the meal tray. "Um, looks pretty good!" I commented. Hungrier than I had had time to think about. "Could I get a large ice water with this?"

"Oh yes sir, I'll get it right away, you famous around here!"

*No, just a crazy old granddad who likes the wind in his hair,* I thought.

After lunch and about 4:00 pm I pushed the white button next to my bed.

"Yes", the nurse replied, how can I help you sir?"

"I was wondering if my X rays were read yet?"

"Oh, I'll check for you."

"Hello, sir. It seems that Dr. Sue Wah Chinn has left for the day."

Oh darn, I remembered. It was Wednesday. Every Doctor's golf day.

"Great," I said, "when can I expect to get out of here then? Listen, I know I have great insurance and I expect you'll want to milk it for the indigents you serve. But I got to get out of here," I inveighed.

"Yes sir, as soon as Dr. Chin releases you." she replied.

"Well you tell Dr. Chin he has a 'chink' in his practice. He shouldn't be leaving this early." Relishing my double enten'dry " "Can I expect to be released by noon tomorrow?" I asked. "Assuming there are no fractures?" knowing that the nurse could not, would not, be able to answer accurately. Too much liability these days.

"Maybe," was her answer.

"Oh, can I get a cup of coffee ?"

"Sure, I'll send it right down to your room."

I had to clear my mind. So much had happened, this day. I really couldn't get started on my little project until I could get to a throw-a-way phone. I didn't have a secure line. I made some notes on the pad in my bedside table.

1. Make contact with Dr. Bremen - Swiss Banker

2. Still into German Bonds? Daws, Clarks, Rheinolbe Unions

3. Still have a contact for Blocking?

4. What is the rate and loan percentage?

5. Best conveyor ?.. Or transfer method. Way to tranuch Swift wire transfer

Here came the coffee. I quickly stuck the pad back into the drawer, as the tray was pushed up to my chin.

"You writt'in to yo girlfriend? Mr. Charles?" the heavy set orderly said.

"Oh no, she left last year when I was away on a business trip."

"Oh, I am sorry to hear that, Mr. Charles."

"Yeah, but she left her two cats to take care of!" I said.

"Oh, dey' alright now that you's in here?"

"Oh yeah, they have a four day feeder and water tower. I am gone a lot."

"That's gute." she said.

I looked away to try and end this conversation.

Well!, to my pleasant surprise my daughter walked into the room. I hadn't seen her in about a month. We lived in the same town.

"Dad! I saw you on TV and it's all over the news. Old man with a white beard, narrowly escapes Tanker blow-up! I talked to the head nurse outside, (She was an RN also) and she says you're are doing fine and 'Where did he get that sense of humor?' How are you really doing ?"

"Oh, just fine," I said. "No worries. But I just barely missed that gas truck! Doing so is what put me into the ditch!"

She looked on, wide eyed with astonishment! "What a mess it was on TV!" she exclaimed, hands waving wildly

"Yeah, that was all behind me."

"Thank God!" she said.

"It was those Country Bumpkin Yea'whoo's that were moving up on my butt to intimidate me. Saw 'em laughing just before I shot around that truck! Truck driver was Texting, I am pretty sure. Sheriff said the boys had done this before. Thought it was funny to intimidate bikers that way. They were cited, last time they did it. The biker was hurt, pretty bad. I was about to become their latest victim.

"Hair, teeth and eyes all over the windshield!, smart asses!, I heard the explosion and felt the heat, but I was looking the other way, down in the ditch. It whooshed over my head. I surmised what happened. I think that truck actually hit my right knee going through the stop sign. You know, I wear that bright Harley Orange vest and helmet."

"Lott'a good that did you!" she asserted.

"Who knows when she hit the brake," I argued.

"Now, the cops have footage from a security camera across the street. I don't think she hit the brake at all. One second sooner and you would have been in the middle of that explosion. You wouldn't have made it."

"Oh well, you all would have had my accident insurance policy in that case."

She slapped me on the shoulder, in protest. "DAD! You have got to stop ridding that Harley. You are too old to be out there!"

"Well, my reflexes surprised even me. Must have had Angel help. Hey it's the only excitement I get these days. You know I am completely alone. It makes me feel alive!"

"You've always lived a little on the edge, but this was close!", she lamented.

"Hey , would you reach into that drawer and give me that little pad, please." I saw that Bobby had left his contact information.

"Who is this?" she asked.

"Just an old friend whose sister is down the hall. I ran into him. We might do a deal together.'

"Yeah, you and your deals, we better get you out of here first."

"All for that," I said.


In came the Channel 9 news person and cameraman. Pretty Blond. "Mr. Charles, can we have a moment of your time?" She shoved the microphone close to my chin. I pulled my sheet up, realizing that the cameraman was closing in on my sagging, hairy boobs. Couldn't have that.

"Sure, I said.

"We saw the security film showing the whole accident. Do you find that people don't respect Motorcycle space often? Mrs. Bollinger pulled right out in front of you."

"I think she was otherwise occupied, ma'am."

"How so". She moved the mike close again.

"Well, I am not for certain, but I could have sworn that she was fooling with her cell phone as she slid through that stop sign. Maybe the film footage will show it." I looked at the cameraman for reassurance.

He nodded.

"Some don't pay enough attention." I looked back at the reporter. "They'll pull right out on you. That's why I wear A bright Orange Harley vest and Orange helmet. Can't miss me coming. But you have to know where to ride in the lane. Out of any blind spot. Proper spacing. And I believe loud pipes make your presence known. It enhances your over-all footprint to the driver's senses, if you will. Some of the Jap bikes are quiet and make very little noise. And you can't be a jerk, cutting in and out of traffic at high speed. Some of the Jap bikes are phenomenally fast, triple the speed limit. Over 200 horses, too fast for other driver's reflexes. Those are the guys that get smeared all over the highway." I glanced over at my daughter. I could tell she was proud of my answers, her head nodding in approval.

The reporter caught my eye shift and moved the mike over to my daughter and asked who she was and was she related to me. She hesitated a second, set back by this sudden attention, looking down the eye of the camera lens now. I laughed out loud at her predicament.

"Hello, I am Kali Anderson and he's my father," she said, shaking her head from side to side. "And he's a wild one, but lucky today," she intoned.

"Well, I'll say." Do you ride a motorcycle too?"

"Oh no, I've got young children to take care of."

She turned her attention back to me, "Do you

think what happened will bring greater attention on the part of drivers to motorcyclist, Mr. Charles?"

"Most countries have many more 'cycles and scooters than we do in the US. Now gas prices are so high, I expect you'll see a lot more sharing the road. Especially Scooters. I hope it increases awareness, but these guys were out for mischief. The Sheriff will tell you they had done this, and were charged, before . A guy was hurt. Not the normal driver inattention, where they were con-cerned. I was just glad I could get out of their way, in time or I'd be down in the morgue, right now."

"Are you sorry for what happened to them," jutting the mike to get my answer.

I thought a minute, realizing I was on TV, and said, "If you can't pay, don't play!"

"Oh Dad!" my daughter exclaimed.

"Hey, they were on a mission, in a three ton ve-hicle, whatt'ah' mean!"

TV lady and cameraman nodded their heads and started to withdraw.

"Hey, I lost my little brother last year, like that. Never found the guy who did it." The cameraman said, with emphasis.

"Sorry to hear that," I said. "I think I got their slant, now."

"Thank you, Sir," was the parting comment from them.

"Well, dad, I gott'a go. Need to feed everybody. They'll be glad to hear you are ok. Maybe we'll be back tomorrow".

"Call first," I said. "I hope to be outt'a here by noon. Just wait'en on an X Ray." Can you pick me up and take me to my car at home? ! I'll take it from there."

"Sure, give me a call. They need to examine your head from the inside out," she laughed and moved toward the door, to leave.

"I did get a little adrenalin rush," I laughed.

She looked at me sternly.

"Tell ya what, I am sure you are right, I am working on a transaction and if it pays out, I promise I'll sell the bike and buy a Corvette convertible. Gott'a be in the air, ya know."

"Well, four wheels are better than two. They're expensive !"

Whew, I laid my head back on my pillow and here came the dinner tray. "Is is that late already?" I said to the orderly.

"Yes sir, came the reply."

I looked back at the contact information left by Bobby for the first time. At the bottom, under his signature, he had written, "Let's do this, Bro." My mind wandered away to a plan.

It was a long night. I finally fell asleep at about midnight. My head was buzzing with plans and fears. The nurse agreed to give me a strong Tylenol to take the edge off everything. I reflected that in a hospital all they will give you is an aspirin and charge you $10.00 dollars a pill. Also 300,000 people die every year from mistakes. Good thing all they can give you is aspirin. Imagine what they could do with a laxative!

Six AM, here come the trays. How could you lose weight in a hospital? You lie on your back and eat all day. "When will Dr. Chinn be in today? Please don't tell me this is his golf day!

"Oh no that's Wednesday," she replied. "I think about 10 AM."

"Hey, my knee feels much better, this morning. Hope to get out of here by noon." I was testing the water. Pincer pressure on all personnel to get me out of here. Once, years ago, I had to just get up and leave because my Doc went home early before releasing me. They don't like that.

Of course, all of these protocols are created and run by the insurance companies. They have to pay out the damages from law suits and in this litigious climate there are lots of them.

I am waiting to see a Kiosk at the exit door,

reading 'Green, Green, Collins and Bernstein'. Two WASP'S, one Irishman, and a Jew, for wide market appeal, "Doubt your Doc... We're on the spot.... For the people, Free consultation."

I imagined a picture of a guy in a three-piece suit with red tennis shoes running to the Court-house, a filing in hand. Oh well, maybe next year. After all, they could advertise now. It made the Yel-low Pages twice as thick. So many trees, so much yellow dye. So many distinguished, white-haired, stately-looking, handsome men with serious ex-pressions denoting accomplishment. Their own wives didn't recognize them after the make-up guy was finished.

Maybe one of those yeh hoos have some kind of an estate. Farm or something, tractor, barn. I could win a lawsuit myself, I considered the prospect. Would be open and shut. Better do an assets test on those guys. Humm, call my 'High-Binder Attorney', tomorrow. Who knows, maybe they own a farm. Not much medical loss, but pain and suffering? Better start moaning, for background.

"Nurse!" I pushed the button. "Concussion!" *This could backfire on my getting out today,* I not-ed.

"Nurse!, Oh, my head hurts, my leg is twitch-ing! I am dizzy, nurse, I think I have a concussion, I am nauseas! My eyes are crossed," I said when she answered. "Did those guys who caused this have any insurance? Is there a record of it?"

"I have no idea, Mr. Charles, but I'll be down in a moment. I just have to stop by the Proctology department first.

"Proctology?" I said. "Whatever for?".

"We have a long, narrow probe that will usually straighten out those crossed eyes quickly," she said. "I'll bring it along."

After a second of contemplation the picture congealed in my mind screen.

"Oh!! Miracle of miracles, what a great hospital you have here! Why, just the healing tone of your voice, the peaceful atmosphere in these hallways. My eyes are straight and 20/20 now! No need for any probes! Praise the Lord, I've been healed!" I shouted.

An old woman in a wheelchair nosed through my door, wide-eyed at the noise. "Hey, sonny, can I get some ah that?"

Amen!

The nurse said, "I'll be right down."

As soon as the nurse arrived, a small man in a white smock came through the door with a large brown envelope in his hand. He walked across the room to the large, rectangular, back-lit light bank, hanging on the wall. He untied a string, reached inside the envelop and withdrew a large negative and slid it up under a clip in the light. "I Dr.

Chinn," he said, with a decidedly Cantonese accent. "This your leg and knee. Look pretty good, just some bruising around knee joint. See fluid, a little swelling. You lucky, Mis'er. Should have mild discomfort for "bout three days. I will give you Naproxen for pain. Nothing broke! You lucky! No ride motorcycle for 2 weeks!" He came over to my bed and took a closer look into my eyes. "You ok, otherwise?"

"Yes, they have been taking good care of me here," I asserted.

"Ah, so! Amazing what Proctology probe fix! Was'a out at Nurse desk when you called in," he winked. "Everything OK?" He smiled and turned to walk out.

"When can I be discharged, Doc?" I said.

"Working on paper work now. This afternoon."

"Oh, good, I exclaimed. I have much to do."

"You take easy for day or two, Mis'er Michael. Close call! Big deal!" He disappeared down the hall.

*** 

"Hi, honey," I called my daughter. "Looks like I'll be released about 3:00, this afternoon. The X Rays were negative. Can you come and get me?"

"Sure, Dad, I can be there at 3:00 for you." "You don't need to come up. "I'll meet you down stairs in the lobby," I said.

"Glad to hear the X rays were alright. How do

you feel otherwise.?"

"Well, a little stiff and sore in places, but I am ok." I assured her.

"Will you be all right home alone?"

Oh, sure, no problem. Hey, I can order a Pizza!" I joked. "Actually, I may be taking a trip out of town on a business matter."

"What?' A trip? Where?"

I didn't want to get into this right now. "Well, it's not for sure, but maybe Amsterdam and then on to the middle East, and back through Switzerland, but don't say anything to anyone else yet."

"Why?" she sounded anxious.

"Well, I don't know the details yet."

"Dad, you're not even out of the hospital yet. When did this come up?" I wanted to spend some time with you."

"That would be great!", I tried to disarm her. "A lot has to fall into place before I would be able to leave, anyway. Passport issues. Visa's to obtain, etc.?

"Where to again, ?"

And I knew I should have kept my mouth shut. "Eventually, Iran."

"IRAN !", she shouted. "Now, when did you come up with this? ah,..., ah, adventure?"

"Sorry, I mentioned it, Honey. Probably won't happen at all. Forget about it. Actually, now that I think about it, it will take a couple a months to arrange."

"Yeah, I remember the last time, when that guy took off for London with your money... Is this one of those deals, Dad? "Does this have anything to do with that Off-Shore Banking stuff?"

"Well, not exactly, honey. Gold Bonds."

Dead silence.

"I don't like the sound of this, Dad. We will talk."

"Oh yeah, plenty of time for that," I said, shifting my feet on the hospital room floor uneasily. I was in for a grilling now and I regretted it "Ok, at three downstairs, then?," I confirmed.

"Yeah, see you then." she said. "I'll pull up under the portico out front."

"They'll probably discharge me from a wheelchair, you know how they do."

"Ok," she sounded a little distant. Concerned.

The orderly came in with paperwork and a wheelchair. He handed me the file and asked for my signature, pointing to an X on a line close to the bottom. "Hey, Cap'tn, look like you are out of here'. It was the young, Navy candidate I talked to earlier.

"Yeah, back on the streets!" I said.

"You be careful now, I'll take you downstairs. You got a ride?" he asked.

"Oh yeah, daughter's coming," I said proudly, as I dressed back into my street clothes from the hospital gown. I glanced around for my phone and those notes left by Bobby. I grabbed a souvenir pen from the drawer to commemorate my two day ordeal, and sat in the chair. Off we went.

My daughter was pulling up outside when I arrived in the lobby.

"Well, here's my ride," I said over my shoulder.

Kali, with a big smile, was just opening the door to take charge. "Hi there! Is he strapped in to that chair?" she joked.

The young man responded, "Actually, we are required to strap patients in the chair," he reached down to unbuckle the chair strap.

"Oh, I know you, didn't you use to work at City General?"

"Yeah, that was a long time ago", he said , now taking a closer look at Kali. "Yeah, you were on the maternity ward, weren't you?"

"Yes. So now you're over here?"

"Yeah, they pay a little better over here," he said by way of explanation.

"Now he is Navy bound," I added, wanting to get into the conversation, gesturing a small salute. "And medical school, I might add."

The young man, with a big smile, reached over my shoulder and shook Kali's hand and said "Jason Richards," to which Kali responded, "Kali Anderson. I am this dare devil's daughter." She shoved me on the shoulder and laughed.

"Well, judging from the TV coverage, he is a lucky guy. Can't say that for the others though," he added. "But hey, he's a young 67, lot's of life left yet."

"Well he always said, it's not the age but the miles that count and at that rate he is about 103!" she added. "Well, it's good to see you again, Jason, and the best of luck with that Navel training."

"Yes ma'am, thank you. Hope to see you again."

There was a commotion at the front desk that was becoming loud. A somewhat tattered middle-aged woman was raising her voice to the reception-ist. "Well, which room is he in?" This Mr. Charles! He done kilt my son Jamie Lee!" She shouted.

They had my attention now. A tall man was standing off to the side, watching me and the order-ly. He saw me look up at him. "Ma, I think that's him over yonder in that wheelchair bout to get out ah here," he said tugging on momma's sleeve, as he took a few steps in my direction. Jason and my daughter sensed the danger. The receptionists was saying, "Ma'am, we can't give out that infor-mation... " now trailing off as the lady—well, more like a dirt bag ol' trailer park lady—turned in my direction with a vicious countenance.

"Oh God!" I heard my daughter say in anticipa-tion. She was a scraper, herself.

"Hey, you the man who crashed my son's truck and kilt him and Josh?"

"No, ma'am, I was in that accident but I barely got around the truck that pulled out in front...," I hadn't finished when she shouted, "I gonn'a sue you for all you got, Mr! Sure as the hogs come in!" she said in pure country drawl.

"Excuse me, ma'am, but all I did was avoid danger. Check with Sergeant Riley. I am afraid your son and his friend were following way too close when that lady—on her cell phone I might add—pulled right out through the stop sign."

"You de only one twat saw that!" she said.

"That's right, that's your lawsuit. Her and the Gas truck company," I added. "So be nice now".

She paused a second for this to sink in.

The tall man interrupted, "Yeah, sis; that's the gas company. They got big bucks! I am sorry for your loss, man, but your recovery is not with me."

She figured it out. I could see it in her face. Relaxing her facial muscles to reveal a toothless grin. Now I was her witness. A ticket to Riche's. "Could you testify to that there, Mr.?" I'd sure be obliged, if you would. Yeah, you got hurt, same as my Jamie," she rationalized.

"I expect I'll have to, ma'am."

A security guard was on hand now, waiting , watching.

"How I know how to get you, Sir?"

"My information is on the police report. Oblivi-ously, I will answer any subpoena, I think I have a case myself. Who knows, ma'am, we may have to enjoin our lawsuits," I said with, I hoped, a disarm-ing smile.

She seemed to relax. She broke into tears, ex-claiming, "Oh! My poor Jamie Lee, I gonna miss that boy, oh."

Her brother went to console her. I nodded at the security guard, indicating I thought the crisis was over. He nodded back and took the chair from Jason, wheeling me through the open doors.

Kali took charge and went through the double doors to her SUV, waiting outside, rear door ajar. I got out of the wheelchair, finally free again now, and got in. It was big and comfortable.

"Wow! I thought that was going to get ugly!" she said, shaking her head.

"Yeah, almost."

"Well, where to, Dad? Kilimanjaro? Montezu-ma? Or Bern?" she joked. "Want a MacDonald's. How about Disney World?"

"Yeah", I laughed out loud, relieved by the hu-mor and freedom. "Well, I want to retrieve my bike from the police impound lot. Sheriff gave me some time without charge and I don't want to go over it."

"OK, well who is going to drive it then.?"

"That's ride it, and I will, naturally."

"Are you kidding me?" she almost shouted as

we pulled from under the portico. Hitting the breaks and upset.

"No problem, honey, we'll go straight home, I promise. I am alright. See, I even have my riding boots on." They still had mud and grass from the ditch. They had been the room closet while in the hospital. A memory flash from seeing the boots.

"Yeah, well, I prefer you drove your Cadillac, for a while, she commented".

"OK, but I got to get it back home and into the garage. Maybe I'll give it to your brother, finally. Been promising him."

"Great idea!" she remarked. "Sonny is much younger than you."

"Oh, hey, pull into that Wal-Mart over there, I need a temporary cell phone. I lost my good one in the wreck," I lied. "I have to be in contact."

She pulled into the lot.

"I am just going to run in quick and grab one."

"Phones are back on the left."

"I'll be right back out. Circle around, these lots are several football fields!"

"OK."

I walked up to electronics and asked for the best temporary, throw-a-way, untraceable cell phone they had. "I want to load it with the maximum minutes. Has to call internationally."

"Yes sir. I've got the Samsung 2103 Trans Atlantic Caller. It has a camera and…" he went on. I stopped him short.

"How much and what can I put on it?" I remembered, that I had three hundred dollars when I started out three days ago.

"The phone is $39.95 and you can put whatever you want on it, sir," was his reply.

"Ok, hey, tell me, will this work in countries like Iran ?"

He looked at me quizzically, "Iran?" he restated.

"Yeah," I said. "I am not a Terrorist, guy, I have a relative…"

He waived me off, "Yeah, it will work there. You know, now they can monitor all signals through the air waves under the Privacy Act or something, anyway."

"Yeah, I know," making a mental note.

"Ok, here's $39.00, tax and two hundred to load on to it. How much a minute, here local."

"Ten cents per minute," he said.

"OK, thanks," gotta run."

The kid watched me move towards the door and reached for his counter phone. He dialed a number.

"Peterson, NSA,: he said.

"Hi, this is Paul Shilling at the phone counter at Wal-Mart."

"Yeah? How can I help you?"

"We were told to report any throwaway phones purchased to you and this guy is asking about IRAN!" he said excitedly. "He was in a real hurry."

"Oh," Peterson said, "Do you have the number assigned at purchase?"

"Yeah, It's 813 654 8091."

"Ok, did he use a credit card?"

"No, he paid cash."

"Any records, at all, like address etc?"

"No," now the counter boy was intrigued all the more, feeling very important at talking with the NSA agent.

"Ok, thanks for your help, Mr. Shilling," and he hung up. He entered the number and a key code for possible future intercept, for "Chatter" surveillance and trace location.

***

I found Kali, just outside the front door and got in. *That went smooth,* I thought to myself.

"OK, ready. Here's the address for the impound lot on the deputy's card. Can you punch it into the GPS, before we get back out into traffic."

"Dad, I can just speak it into the unit." she said. "Yours is old, this one is in the dash from the factory."

"Ok, well, speak it, then girl." I laughed. "Don't want another accident, you know. Need to get there before 5:00."

Little did I know, I had already been compromised. Not only whatever conversations I had but a GPS tracking embedded in the phone would disclose my travel and where a bouts!

"OK, here we are," as we pulled up to the impound lot.

I went inside and asked for my keys. The deputy checked his record and said, "No charge, sir." He went behind a barrier and returned with my keys. "It's out back. I'll unlock the gate for you, sir."

I walked outside and around to the gate. The deputy opened the gate and pointed over to a far corner where I could just make out my Harley. It used to be spotless, white pearl but looked a little different now. Mud and grass were caked and dried on the side. The handlebars were a little twisted, the mirrors bent and the horn, usually mounted on the left side, was gone. My luggage packs were all askew and mud and water stained but the rims weren't bent so if it would start, I could ride it home. On second thought..., I pulled out my wallet and reached in the back fold for my "Harley Handy" insurance card. *Wait a minute*, I thought. *This is what I pay for! Have them tow it to the dealer for repairs. It is looking pretty sorry right now.*

I looked for the deputy to ask how late they were open but he was nowhere in sight. I pulled my card, whipped out my new phone and dialed the number. "Harley Handy" came the answer. "Do you have a claim today?"

"Hi, yes I do. Here is my policy number."

Oh, I see a 2003 Harley, full coverage."

"Yes, ma'am, I was involved in an accident two days ago. I was just released from the hospital and I need the bike towed to the dealer for repairs."

"Where is the bike now?" she asked.

"It's at the Sheriff's impound lot on 21st and Central Avenue under my name. I know it's late today but tomorrow morning will be fine. It will go to Biscayne Harley on Route 1. I'll call ahead and notify them. See Mr. Foster when you drop it off. He'll know what to do."

"All right, Mr. Charles, our tow will pick it up and our agent will meet a Mr. Foster at the dealer to estimate the damages."

"You know, you guys are so easy to work with. Thank you."

"So glad to give you good service, Mr. Charles. Will there be anything else?"

"Oh yeah, whatever is replaced, please use Harley factory replacement parts."

"Oh yes, always, Mr. Charles."

I hung up and began walking to the car. Kali had parked it and was walking towards me.

"Did you find it?" she asked.

"Oh yeah, over there." I waved.

"Oh my God, Dad. That's it? It's a wonder you

weren't hurt!"

"Yeah, matter of fact, a change in plans. I am having it towed to the dealer."

"Oh great, makes sense to me. "Tell 'em to keep it!" Do we have to wait?"

"No, I told them tomorrow would be fine. Hey, I'll take you to dinner, if you have time."

"Sure."

Chapter 3

Lunch With My Daughter

Walking to the car she said, "Let's go to 'Jimmy Crack Claw', "I feel like seafood and it's close. And it's Stone Crab Season."

"Sounds good to me," I said, looking forward to this event with my daughter. She was busy with advanced nursing school and I just didn't see her much these days. Oh, I could taste the Rum and Coke I was looking forward to. A little buzz and relaxation. All business down, for now.

"OK, only broad strokes, right now. Nothing set or gelled as yet, but basically, I ran into an old friend while in the hospital. Just by chance. Bobby is a nephew of the Reza Palavi, the former Shah of Iran. This was before your time," I added. "The United States Government was an ally of the Shah and gave him asylum back then. Late 50's- early 60's. There was a revolution and a coup. Quick exit. Well, it turns out that Bobby, Alias Buruse Bacthier, The Royal Family, was left a stack of those German Gold Backed Bearer Bonds I used to deal in years ago in a safety deposit box back there from before WWII. I don't know what issues they are but are most likely, very valuable. These bonds are known to exist by elements of the current regime and an offer has been made to liquidate or utilize them in some way, with the promise of rewards and riches."

"So, where did you run into this Bobby?", she inquired with appropriate cynical curiosity.

"Ya know, when I got into my room at the hospital, his sister was in the room next door. He poked his head in by mistake, you know how close those rooms are together. Of course, there was a lot of commotion in my room with the Deputies, etc and I recognized him from the 80's . He asked me if I was still involved with the bonds in a general conversation of re-acquaintance. So he mentioned the bonds he had inherited and wondered about their present day value. I told him ,possibly a million apiece. They are Art objects, Artifacts, in addition to their appreciated gold value. I would have to see them.

"He said he had been approached to investigate their value and proceed with a possible plan of redemption."

"OH! Now, let me see if I understand. You are talking about recovering millions of dollars worth of Gold Backed Bearer Bonds in Iran, in some kind of redemption scheme with those crazy people? They will cut your throat in a second when they have a 'Bearer Bond in hand and they don't need you anymore! You are in way over your head! They are building centrifuges to refine weapon-grade uranium right now, to threaten us, Israel and the rest of the world!" Are You Nut's?

"NO, No, you don't understand. It will all be done offshore in a Swiss Account." I retaliated.

"Yes, but you have to physically get to the bonds first. They are "Bearer" bonds. Do you see the vulnerability."

"I will transfer serial numbers first. And then a super secure transfer agent."

"Yes," she interrupted, "but at some point you must physically remove the bonds from wherever they are located and you are talking billions. You better have the Virgin Mary and her crew, St. Michael and Leonardo Deviancy for your transfer crew." She really believed she would never see me again. I would not survive this adventure. "How's your Farsi?"

There was 'Always Transmit' setting on the surveillance system tray for tracking. It enabled 24 hour, constant, voice-activated, speech transmission. This feature provided all voice transmission recording. Any conversation whether a call was transmitting or the phone was off! The technician activated it. I was already on the "General Interest" inquiry level of surveillance protocol. Of course, I was unaware of this or the capabilities of the current technology. It was Top Secret. My observation footprint included the NSA, the CIA, the FBI and the State Department and, with Allied Treaties: Israel, Western Europe and Australia. They could be co-opted in by switching a switch on a defense satellite.

We were seated right away and were about to order drinks,

"So, tell me about your latest deal to these distant places."

*Oh, Hell*, I thought.

Here was the waiter, "Yes sir?"

I was glad for the convenient interruption. "We'll each have your Crack Claw special with garlic dip on the side, please, and what would you like to drink today, I looked at my daughter, inquiringly.

"I'll have a 'Risky Business', please."

"Oh," I said, "I'll have one of those also, please.

"Hey, good choice, what's in it?" I asked.

"It's a high risk cocktail. It has about four white liquors and is laced with Single malt scotch. If you're not careful, it may blow up on you!"

"Very funny, I've never had one."

"Yes you have; oh, you mean the drink!" She

laughed.

"Tell you what, I will clear this at all levels. Banking, travel agency, maybe my buddy at State."

"Oh, yeah, State. They will be thrilled." She commented. "I still don't like it."

Here were the drinks and we each took a long draft of the, tall, cool, ice covered tumbler.


Reflection; Just two days ago, I was peacefully ridding my motorcycle down the two-lane highway, in town—this town—and in a few seconds, there was kayos. Three people were dead and I was contemplating going to one of the hot spots, politically, speaking, in the world, sitting here drinking something called " Risky Business. *Am I missing something? I wondered. When I finish this drink, the anticipatory anxiety butterflies in my stomach will go away, I hope.*

*Oh! That is good! Those butterflies came out my ears! This "Risky Business sure brings a rosy glow!* It was a 2 for 1, so I was going to have to have another before I left. *Oh, pain and suffering!* "How is your drink?" I asked Kali.

"Pretty good. It sure does the job," she said.

"I noticed," I replied as I stretched out a little, anticipating those 'Claws'.

"You know, Dad, you are 67 years old now."

I checked my lapel and said, "Right!"

"Ha, Ha! I mean you have to slow down a little.

You came inches away from being killed the other day."

"You know the slogan, 'Ride to live, Live to ride'," I said.

"Yeah, that's how Harley sells motorcycles. How about those who ride and die?"

"Isn't that what makes it exiting?" I teased. We had been through this dialog before, same result.

"Really, what makes it so desirable ? I think it has something with anti-gravity. Humans, at the root of it, want to fly. The feeling of gliding though the air with nothing around you and the power thrust from the torque of the motor, coupled with the sound of the compressed air escaping through the air in a punctuated staccato crescendo of escaping burnt gases, all the while, leaning into centrifugal force and working multiple controls and levers, pedals and shifters, I mean think about it. It's a male's mega toy! Zoom, Zoom! And when you are 67 years old, it smacks of a grip on eternity. And then there's the cult.

"Hats, boots, leathers, shirts, belt buckles, pins... It's marketing genius! I mean. don't they ride these in the afterlife?" I offered.

She said "Sure, Dad, the 'J.C. Riders'; their leathers are out of this world!"

We had a good laugh.

"Well, that was a special time. After that second 'Risky Business', I need to risk some nap time. Can you take me to my condo now? And I have some calls to make."

We pulled out into the busy street. I didn't notice the dark grey sedan that pulled out from the curb and followed us.

"Subject moving," was the radio call.

"This is light surveillance," came the reply. "Just interested in a residence, if you can get it."

"Roger that."

We pulled up under the covered entry of my condo. I was on the 9th floor of a nice, glass building called The Mansions. I was located right on the Beach. Great view of the town. The tail car drove right by and reported my address back to his controller.

"Well, I enjoyed lunch, honey. Those Claws were a hit and thanks for picking me up from the hospital. I am going to take a little nap. I will see you later in the week."

"OK, Dad. I love you."

"Love you, too. Kiss the grandkids for me."

I walked towards the elevator and ran into Dennis, the building commentator of all information flowing through the air ways. It was a calling for him. "Hey, Mr. Charles! How you doing? I saw you on the TV. You look pretty good for what you went through."

"Actually, I was ahead of the mess and went into the ditch. I think it protected me from the blast."

"I was goanna come visit at the hospital but now you're out."

"It was nothing, just an X ray for the knee and leg, everything was OK."

"That's good, you were lucky. Don't ya think you ought to give up that motorcycle at your age?"

"What, and give up all this excitement?"

"Well, you take it easy now," as he scurried out to the pool deck to pass on the news he had gleaned to the loungers. We were a pretty close group of neighbors.

I pressed 9 on the elevator. Just before the door closed an unfamiliar gentleman came through the opening, "10" he said when I reached for the panel offering to press his floor. I hadn't seen him before and thought him a visitor. Being located on the beach, we had many visitors. I got off at 9. I thought he watched while I went to my door, but figured it was just my imagination. I was just off the elevator, reaching for my key.

Ah!, it was good to be home. I walked over and surveyed the beach from the 9th floor as I attempted to focus on where I had put those files from years ago. They contained some contacts I would need. Thank God for my German ancestry in that we were careful to keep records. I was a Rommal on my mother's side, that was "el" instead of "al" but we were related back to the famous Field Marshal of North Africa. *Let's see, The large brown box in the second bedroom closet,* I thought. *Would they still be alive,* I wondered. I dug through and soon found what I was searching for. I would have to wait until three AM my time to make the call when the Swiss Bank opened. I lay down for a nap.

At 3: AM, after a strong cup of coffee.

"Ellow, this is the Bank of Switzerland, how may I direct your call?"

"Hello, is a Dr. Bern still at your bank?"

" Villiam or Heinz?"

"Ah, the older one, I imagine."

"That would be Heinz.May I tell him who is calling?"

"Yes, I am Michael Charles, an old contact.

"One moment, please," came the reply.

I couldn't believe my luck. "Executive Office of Dr. Heinz Bern, who is calling, please?"

"Michael Charles, a former contact. He may not remember, it's been some years... regarding German Gold Bonds."

"Hello?" came an almost immediate response.

"Dr." Bern?" I said.

"Yes, I am Dr, Bern. Heinz Bern. How can I help you, sir."?

"Dr. Bern, you will  no doubt not remember,

but about 10 years ago you helped me with some gold bonds. We Blocked them against a credit line to invest into a US Federal Roll Program."

"Ya," came the reply, "Michael!" he exclaimed loudly. "I remember, of course, I remember! How have you been, young man?"

"Well, getting along, I guess." Ah, the inevitable small talk.

"And vhat are you doing now?"

"Well, sir, I have some German, Gold Backed, Bearer bonds from WWII that have been locked up in a safety deposit box since the end of the war. I am wondering about their value."

"Oh, could they be authentic? How many?"

"Several stacks depending on current value assessment, perhaps 10 billion."

"Oh, Michael, where could so many still be located?"

"Do you remember Reza Pahlavi?"

"Yes, de Shah of Iran."

"Well, they were in the estate of Reza Pahlavi and left to his Grand nephew, in a lock box all these years."

"Really, could this be true? These are Bearer bonds. Their government will want them back. The Shah stole millions of dollars. How would you get them out from Iran, I assume that is where they are?

"The nephew , a longtime friend of mine, has a

"Conveyance" to travel inside the country and secure them."

Dr. Bern laughed heartily, out loud. "Oh Michael, They will never allow you to leave alive. Those bonds are extremely valuable if authenticated. Don't be foolish and remove them from your hiding for that regime. You are a dead man!" He went on."

"Well, actually, they have co-opted the nephew with a plan to convert them to useable cash through a credit facility. This is why they will let us travel out."

"To where?"

" To you, of course."

"Oh, Michael, I am too old for this! So much intrigue, so much danger. There would be disclosures needed."

I could tell he was interested as he went through the mental exercise, There was a fortune to be made in this blocking and sale of series notes on Top 25 Western European Banks, to investors around the world at various discounts.

"Dr. Bern, I will be taking the physical risk until I show up at your door with the physical bonds."

"You will never make it here, Michael. You would need world-class, first-order security protection."

"Yes, well, I wanted to ask you about that. Who do you know?"

"This would be very expensive, maybe $300,000 USD."

"Ok, if they can wait until after we get the bonds blocked up. You would advance that amount, wouldn't you?"

"Oh, Michael, I just don't know. I must consider all of this. Can you call me tomorrow, at say noon, my time?"

"Sure, it was good talking to you again. I see your son is working at the bank now."

"Ya, Ya," he said. "I am getting old. I need to retire. I have dat Chalet in the Alps, you know, I'd like to ski again, while I still can."

Dr. Bern had invited me over to Switzerland the last time we were doing business, for a wonderful week of skiing back in the late 90's, breath taking beauty. "Yes, I remember, Heinz. That was very special, I remember it well."

"Ya, Ya." He had been like a warm granddad to me.

"I will call another bank. We might need some group help for the amount I think you will need if these serial numbers are authentic."

"Good, Doctor, they have never been moved."

"Ok, Next week."

"Ok." Before he hung up he added, "Are you sure you know what you are getting yourself into, Michael? There may be some very dangerous characters involved. With this much money, you're dead very soon if something goes wrong."

"Got it! I will take your 'Q' on security. Do you know of a top notch firm?"

"Vill check."


I hung up and called my old travel agent. "Border Jumpers," came the answer.

"Hey, you guys have a lot competition in the South West USA, don't you!"

"Oh no, we have luxury Bus with full service. How can I help you?"

"This is an old customer, Mike Charles and I need to know what' all hoops I need to jump through to travel two people, from here to Tehran, Iran, for 2 day stay and return through Bern, Switzerland , with a two day layover in Switzerland. Four star hotels will do and regular class airfare or whatever they call that these days."

"Do you have a passport? And how about a visa?"

"Yes and no on the visa, not yet."

"When are you planning to travel, Mr. Charles? Oh, I see your record now. We have your credit card on file. Is it the same account number?"

"Yes," and traveling early next month, tentatively ."

"Well, let's see, that's a mouthful. Can I work on this and call you back"?

"Sure, same number as in your file."

"You may need an invitation from the Iranian government, though to, clear."

"Will a fax authorization be sufficient for you?" I asked.

"Yes, if it is on official stationary from their Travel Ministry."

"OK."

I rubbed my hands together. *Now we making some progress,* I assured myself. *Next call in the morning, Bobby King.* I checked for his information from the hospital drawer. I still had it in my pants pocket.

"Hello?"

"Hey, Bobby! How you doing ? It's Mike."

"Oh, are you are home already or still in the hospital?"

"No, home. No problems."

"Ah, that's good, man."

"Listen, I have made some preliminary calls to the bank in Switzerland to feel out my contact. He will call back after he attempts to line up some participation. That's a lot of money, you know."

"Yeah, man."

"Look, do you know how dangerous this could be? I keep getting warned."

"I think my contact can protect us, and guarantee safe passage," he said.

"You sure?"

"Yes, they are loyal to my family."

"Ok, if you say so. I am lining up security for the Switzerland leg of the trip, actually, now that I think of it, they should take us out of Iran. Plan on about $300,000 grand, all told."

"Wow!"

"Ok, Bobby, these could be worth billions! That makes for strange bedfellows. And loyalties. We do want to get back, you know." We can send the proceeds by Swift secure wire Traunch from Switzerland but may be vulnerable until then."

"So what did he say?"

"Well he needs to authenticate the serial numbers but if they are authentic, we are probably a go. Who is the money going back to, anyway? After our commission, of course. What have you been offered to complete the transaction?"

"Half and I am splitting that with you."

"Do you know what it will be used for?"

"All I know is infrastructure," he said.

"Hell, that could be anything.

The young corporal, ripped off his headphones and moved to the voice transmission printer in the surveillance room at the Pentagon. *What did I just hear? This is going to the Colonel immediately! We have just gone from level 4 security, general priority surveillance, to level 2 Alert status, which must be reported to several agencies, now! Iran - Bil-*

*lions - Infrastructure - sounds like centrifuges to me,* he thought. *A Yellow cake bonanza! Of course, Yellow cake is euphemistic for refined, weapon-grade Uranium. Holy Crap!*

He pulled the sheet and ran to Colonel's Bullock's door. "Colonel, Sir!, I think you should see this right away!"

"What is it, Corporal?"

"It's a surveillance print out of those two guys, screwing around with Iran. They are planning a trip over there! And on to Switzerland."

"Turns out one of them is a nephew of the former Shah, you remember, Reza Pavli and he was left an inheritance of some German Bonds worth major bucks, Sir. Billions! They are working through a Swiss Bank to liquidate them and use the proceeds to enhance their refinement efforts in Theater."

"Let me see," the colonel reached for the red sheet.

"Nothing is set as yet sir. Just preliminary inquires, travel agent, banking forays, etc. Sir, do you know what they could do with that kind of money, Iran, I mean?" More Centri...."

The colonel finished his sentence, "fugue's. Ok, I'll move this forward to General Reed in the Joint Chief's office and Sec. State surveillance alert periphery for further observation. You stay on the thread, Corporal. Good Work, Son.

"Hello, Ms. Daniels, This is Colonel Bullock. I am sending a top priority Scan, secure, to General Reed. Please give it to him right away."

"Yes sir ,Colonel. Will do. Right away, Sir.

Col. Bullock, under his breath, was barely heard to murmur, *"Those little punks are in way over their heads, they'll never make it out of there alive."*

A button was pressed and several top secret receiving locations were activated.

Phone ringing... 6 AM came quickly after my 3: AM call to Dr. Bern.

"Hello, Mike? Bobby. Hey, I just talked to my man in Tehran. He said commercial air travel was way too risky. If we can get to Amsterdam, he will send a private jet to take us to Tehran to retrieve the bonds and onto Switzerland to the bank."

"Ok, but we have to have our security with us all the way. Nobody else, but the pilots. The pilots must remain locked in their flight deck with one of our security guys watching the flight deck door."

"Really, man?" Bobby replied.

"Listen, man, these are bearer bonds worth enough money to turn anybody into a thief. Our security works for the Bank. They won't know what we have in the package. Who won't kill you for hundreds of millions of dollars?" I exclaimed.

"Wow, I see, I am just beginning to comprehend the gravity here. You are right, this is getting a little scary."

"Better to be scared than sorry. We have to be vigilant until they are in the hands of Dr. Bern and signed for. All serial numbers receipted."

"Yeah, I seem man, hey, you got it!"

"Remember, the credit facility proceeds will be sent by Swift Secure Wire Traunch".

"How do we get paid after that?"

"Better think about it," I said. "I suggest we send a net Traunch so that we have our cut out first before we send the proceeds from the bank. Tell your guy. He will be asked to authorize this in writing to the Bank and Dr. Bern as a condition of transfer."

"Ok, I can get that, man," Bobby, breathing heavily.

"Insist on it! "We have to protect ourselves every step of the way." I added.

Bobby responded, "I see, I see."

"You keep thinking that way! I getting a drink!" Slightly broken English.

"I am going to be in D.C. next week. Can you meet me there. I'd like to go through a kind of rehearsal summary of all our plans."

"Yeah, I can be there. Where"?

"Say, the Mall. Just take the Metro from Springfield to the main station and on to the Mall.

I'll meet you outside the Smithsonian, the old red building at 12:00 on Tuesday. We'll go to a bench where we can see all around us.

"Sounds good, man. I can be there."

Corporal Donovan was writing furiously, even though he had recording surveillance in place. He wanted to make a favorable impression on Col. Bullock. *Another trip to his office and eyeball contact couldn't hurt. I want a career.*

"OK," as he scanned the report. "I want dish mic, long-distance pick-up on that bench," was athe Colonel's only comment.

"Yes Sir, I'll see to it through 'Stake Out', on Tuesday at 12:00, Sir; the Red Spire bench location.

I was in an altered state of alerted conscience now as I scanned, projected, role-played, debated and asked myself what could go wrong. What were the possibilities? I needed to feel like I could brief our security people, but of course, they would know their job well.

This is what happens when you are a control freak, I reflected.

Always a geography nut, I went to my large National Geo Atlas and scanned the area. I wanted to know the terrain. I saw a small municipal airport, close to the city. We wouldn't want a hassle with an

International facility with those bonds. Karaj, General Aviation Airport. *That's the one we'll use.*

I made a mental note to call `Border Jumpers` and make the change to our itinerary to exclude the second leg to Tehran from Amsterdam. And to call Dr. Bern to get our security on board our flight from Amsterdam.

When I called, Dr. Bern simply gave me the name of the chief of security to liaison with for my needs and changes to our plans. "Michael, can you text me one serial number of the stack as soon as you can get it? I need to verify for my file and these security expenses."

"Will do', Heinz, as soon as I have them in our car."

*Time to go lay on the beach and reflect. Let's see Bathing suit, sandals, large towel, lotion and radio. OK, think that's it. Heading for the elevator.* A tall blond woman rounded the hallway corner as I stepped out of my door, "Oh excuse me" as I almost bumped into her.

"Oh, sorry, sir. I don't know where I am going. Can I get to the beach down this elevator?"

"Oh yes," I said, glad to help her out. "This will let you out on the left porch downstairs. With the offset towers, there is a shadow on the right side. That's the nicest side of the building for sun this time of the day. new here?"

"Yes, I am visiting the Goldberg's, upstairs."

Of course, she was younger than I was, isn't everyone, but very pleasant to look at. Her hair was pulled back over her left ear, revealing a small mole, just behind it. I made a mental note on the way down to the deck.

"Here we are," I said, "just down the hall to the left and through that door, ma'am".

"Oh thank you, my name is Jennifer; ma'am sounds so old."

"Hi, Jennifer, I am Mike Charles. Nice to meet you." I took a bottle of cold water off of the serving window ledge and left a dollar in the cup, dropped three steps to the beach and headed closer to the salt water. Oooo, the sun felt good! What a scene, there was a hang parachutist hanging overhead, pulled by a speed boat, a couple of surfer's, a `Hobe Cat` breaking the waves., two Jet Skier's and some distant kettle music, This was a great place to live!

There were two buildings located right on the beach. They sat unfinished for several years. The builder went bankrupt and left them sitting; two giant hulks, with no windows. Just poured concrete floors, and support columns. A bit of a blight on the beach. Then one day, John Syme came along, a local developer. The market had changed, and he decided to divide each floor into only four large units.

He used glass panels which reached from the floor to the ceilings and called the buildings, 'Mansions By The Sea'. They were large and unique. They were a hit. I was on the ninth floor, and the city was lit at night below for a great view. To compliment that, I completely mirrored one wall in the living room to reflect he outside image. Well, the corner columns in effect, disappeared, It was like floating in the air on the ninth floor, lights and ocean all around. So festive, a great place to return to after traveling the East coast most of the week, from Cape Cod , Virginia, South Carolina, and Florida.

I dozed off on the beach towel. I must have been really worn out. When I awoke, the sun was setting over the sea. A little groggy, I went to the outside shower and rinsed off in the cold water. Wow!

A Hawaiian guy was just tuning up at the pool bar. *Why not?* I thought. I went by and ordered a Strawberry daiquiri. They made a great one at our pool bar. Fresh fruit. Ice in a blender, Cindy did a great job. After all, isn't this what it was all about? He started up with a Jimmy Buffet tune. *That'll keep me here a while,* I thought, tapping my foot. I pulled out my phone and called Border Jumpers' Agency. "Hello, Michael Charles here, I need to change my itinerary."

"All right , Mr. Charles, and what changes?".

"Well, I am still not certain of a departure date but I need to cancel the leg from Amsterdam to Tehran. I'll call John later on with a certain date for travel,".

"Ok, Mr. Charles. Thanks for calling us back"

Tuesday came before I knew it. I arose at 5 AM and headed out to DC. It was a 3 hour drive. I dressed casually in Kakis and a pink Colombia fishing shirt. *Forget the Caddy, I am taking the Corvette on this ride, this early.* Zoom, it came to life. Throaty, stainless exhaust—it echoed under the building Garage. It had a covered berth underneath that I rented to keep the salt and sand off its red paint job. *Now, Michael, No tickets,* I told myself. Errrt, the tires squealed. Well, you know how those polished concrete floors are! *Too early,* I told myself. These people aren't up yet. It was about 30 minutes to the interstate highway where I could really make some time.

I hit the on-ramp with anticipation. As soon as I negotiated the curve and was heading straight, I goosed it in second gear, right up to 6,500 RPM, then shift to third, then 4th. Whoa!, I was already doing 85 and that was over the limit. 2 gears to go! I backed off. There would be plenty of traffic coming up soon enough. This baby was soo smooth! I was thinking about how I might put that to the officer if he stopped me and reminded myself that the car was expensive enough. I didn't need tickets to boot. Tickets were very high, these days. All State Governments were burdened with FBL's (Fat Black Ladies) from the affirmative action days and now it was their pensions, health costs and retirement benefits that were straining budgets all over, but especially in the East region.

"Oh Jesus, I could go to jail for that thought." "Yes, Miss Beulah, No, I was just kidding! Whap!, No no don't hit me no moe, Miss Beulah! Don't hits me no moe!" I was old enough to remember The Amos and Andy Show. I had to laugh out loud. *It was great to be able to entertain yourself,* I thought. You couldn't say that today.

Now I was not prejudice mind you, I had three beautiful mixed-blood grand children whom I loved dearly. I had spent a great deal of time with my granddaughter and she was the apple of my eye. As Dr. Martin had said, *'It's the content of their character. Not the color of their skin!'* Although, I thought some laws passed over the last 20 years had swung the pendulum a little too far. Well, that was normal pendulum dynamics. I was always pleased and proud when I ran across a young black man who was successful and not an opportunistic, Jelly Bean, High Pocket's slim, shuck and diver! Those guys ended up in the system. But, you know,

the sad thing is because of their sub-cultural pro-
clivities and exposures, lack of role models in the
household, they didn't have a chance without a lot
of TLC. And Momma was usually working and
didn't have time to give it. I thought this change  is
going to take several more generations, but much
progress has been made. Sports or education was
their way up. My mind wandered. My only prejudice was not skin color but behavior. Whatever the
color of the person's skin.

*These days, there were camera's everywhere.
And a red car..... No way ! Heading to D.C., I'll bet
there's an "Eye in the Sky watching me right now!*
I was very careful to keep it one mile under the limit, which led me to reflect upon why I'd bought such
a fast car for so much money. *Second childhood, I
guess. But then the first was wild enough! Good
thing I didn't fly anymore! I had to grin.*

Oh sure, now you're just chasing Bearer Bonds
into one of the hottest spots in the world. I could
hear my daughter say. 'A place you really don't
know much about'. I had about 2 ½ hours left to
think about what all could go wrong. I didn't realize
that the grey suit on the elevator and the tall blond
were keeping me company the whole way, close behind. It was then that I remembered, the Shah was
more or less extracted and rushed into asylum by

the US government. He was thought to have stolen millions from the people. Even though Bobby had inherited legally, they would probably want to confiscate anything discovered left behind. Better bring that up with Bobby.

Getting closer to the city now, the early morning rush hour was thick. *Glad I made it for noon,* I thought. "Hey Bobby!, you up?" I said to the mellow voice that answered the phone.

"Yeah".

"Good, I am heading into the city now. I will go to the Willard for a bit of breakfast and see you at 12:00 on the Mall."

"Yeah, central exchange to the front of the Smithsonian, right.?"

"You got it. Bring any papers you've got."

"Like"...? "

"Passport, bank location, safety deposit key, ID for the bank, anything you think we might need. This is a dry run. We can't get over there and forget something here! Put your thinking cap on and take yourself through every step."

"Ok, man, I see."

"Good. We'll talk on the Mall at 12:00. See you then."

I could taste that breakfast at the Willard. It was always great. They set out a buffet that was killer! And I was Hungry. *Now don't get all loaded down with carbohydrate's. Potatoes, pancakes, Biscuits and all. You'll need a nap from hypoglycemia and wont be worth a damn, by noon. You need to be sharp! Maybe just a breakfast steak. Marinated in Grey's chutney and charcoaled with a little Château Laffite Rothschild, Burgundy, on the side.* The chef knew what I liked. That was my standard, years ago. *Oh, it's hell to get old,* I thought as I remembered those Halcyon days. *Where did I think I was, New Orleans?*

"Good morning sir., can I get you some coffee?"

"Sure and please tell Chef George that 'Ol Mike Charles' will have the chef's 'Texas Wake-up', medium rare, please. He is still here, isn't he?"

"Oh yes, sir. Morning 'till night."

"Good, that'll do it. I know you don't serve Château Laffite by the glass, so I'll have a small split of Pies porter, chilled."

"Yes sir. Will that be all?"

"Yes, think so."

Across the large dining room, I thought I recognized a gentleman in a grey suit. I knew I had seen him before, but I didn't know him. *Where, Where?,* I asked myself, straining to remember. I thought, *Was that the little guy in my elevator the other day? Oh no, what are the chances.* I dis-

missed it, thinking it too improbable. Another gentleman sat at his table and began an animated conversation. They didn't look my way, so I dismissed
it. Here was my steak anyway.

*Great breakfast! Think I'll go by the gift shop
on my way out.* I passed by the grey suit and I just
couldn't shake it. The man at his table had a dis-
tinct bulge under his coat on the lower right waist-
line. Was he armed? Well, this was Washington DC
after all, likely some form of law enforcement or
Government enforcement. Nobody else could pos-
sess a handgun in this city. They didn't look at me,
and I just passed by.

I used to run these streets as a teenager; a
young fellow trying to be dapper. Full of visions
and imaginary scenarios what could be ahead. I
had been in some of the finest homes in the city because of my father's business. He catered to the
carriage trade. Been in the homes of some major
press personalities. A ballroom cotillion at the Con-
gressional Country Club, a young man invited to
Lyndon Johnson's table. The concert piano at the
British Embassy just before the Ambassador's
wife's luncheon, playing 'boogie woogie' while the
Mrs. Ambassador came screaming out of the Chan-
cery door, "Get that young man out of here Oh, get
that young man out of here!" Boy did I run down

those red-carpeted, white marble staircases in a hurry. I was only 15. In retrospect, I don't think those Spanish service personnel really understood when I asked if I could play the piano.

Now, almost 50 years later it seemed like such a long time ago. And, then, there was the USIA. A big contract for the business dad owned. You'd be amazed what you see when no one's around and you're not a threat to anyone. I had been running the hallways of government building since 1948. Mom worked for selective service. She was the gal you went to see when your number came up. Your draft number, that is.

I turned into the gift shop, looking for some memento of the old Willard Hotel, to take back home. A focal piece to introduce all the old stories to my grandchildren. Or maybe not.

I decided to leave my car at the Willard and take a cab to the nearest Metro station., then the Metro to the Mall outside the Smithsonian, Red Building.

I was always impressed when I popped out from underground to sunshine in the middle of the National Mall amid all the Museums that lined both sides of the street with the Washington monument right in the middle. In my day our primary education celebrated American History. There was statuary of those people we studied all over the city. We said the pledge of allegiance every morning and the US Flag was venerated. Your country was everything! All the best virtues and values were practiced. Truth still mattered. There was no such thing as "Situational Ethics" back then. The rule book was much simpler. "Be straight and don't be late."

Everyone today haz some agenda, an "Alter Isness", smoke and mirrors, shell games and the leaders were among the worst offenders. Had they ever voted themselves government largess! Our current president took more vacations than a travel agency owner! Some valued at 10's of millions of dollars. 5 million just for the dog! Makes you want to get lost in the Rocky Mountains! Boone and Crocket, Regan, where are you when we need you?

I hailed a cab. "Metro," I said, 'Nearest station, please." We pulled away. I noticed through the driver's rear view mirror, the Grey suit hailed a cab right behind me 300 feet. I was certain it was him. He was alone. *Too much coincidence!*, I thought. *Who cares*? I thought, *I am not doing anything wrong. If I see this guy again I am going to offer him my Hanky for its scent!* We caught a quick traffic light, and he with a red, fell back.

Now, at the station, I pulled my small digital Nikon out of my inside pocket. Very slim profile. I wanted to look like a tourist. Plus , the Mall was always good material.

I will never tire of it. Up the 3 story escalator and Whoosh! Sunshine and the National Mall all around you. Capital Building at one end and Lincoln at the other. So much history had taken place here since 1948. All the memories, Cherry Blossoms to Nam and the new WWII memorial. Many 4 of July's and a few concerts. Great restaurants and three martini lunches. Commuter flights to New York, cheap, for a celebratory lunch, back by dinner. What a great city to grow up in. Eat your heart out, Igor!

I made my way down to the park bench we had agreed to meet on. It was empty. Good. I was just a little early and started taking some pictures, like Tommy tourist. Wow, these downtown DC working women were good looking.

Here came the big smile. Laughing, singing, swinging arms, Bobby strolling down the river rock covered pathway. He had a wild looking hat on. Purple.

"Hey, yo! Aren't you a sight dude!" I had to say.

"Ya, Man, no worries," he came back. "How you doing?"

"Good man, but I think I am being followed."

Ah, man, you're crazy! Are you paranoid"?

"No, just careful" A guy I saw in my elevator in my condo showed up for breakfast 3 hours away. How's that for coincidence"?

"So, did you give him a donut?"

"No, but I should have. Look, Bobby, this deal has the potential of attracting various interests. Every day, we hear about new invasions to our privacy. People are listening. That's why I choose this bench to talk on. Here's the thing. Bearer Bonds belong to whoever has a hold of them, Hence, the Bearer. Yours could be worth hundreds of millions."

"Yeah man," he rubbed his hands together.

"You are dealing with a country very hostile to the U.S. I really want you to concentrate on the gravity of this transaction."

"Man, I see. Those people are still pretty backward, you know.".

"Yeah, but you can pull a trigger going forward or backward," I admonished, smiling.

"Ok , what up?"

"Ok, do you have your passport all up to date? Are your safety deposit ID and key in place. We are gonn'a be thousands of miles away. We can't just come home and get it. Do you have all important "Permission" letters you might to satisfy customs. How about 'Will and Testament' papers if they become necessary.?"

"Ok, Ok, yeah, I see. I will put everything in my

brief case including the kitchen sink! No, you are right!"

"Now, I've cancelled the Iraq leg of the trip with the travel agency. Did your man agree to have our security team on the plane and the pilots' door locked?"

"Yes, but we won't have the bonds yet." Why would they..."

"Just trying to be careful. Wann'a get overpowered and forced to give up your key, etc. ?"

"Ya! You slick, alright, think of everything!"

"Try to. Remember, the rabbit that jumps never gets shot!"

"Ha!, you so funny, Mike"

"Let me ask you, How many of your countrymen would you trust with your millions?"

He thought for a second, "Not even my mother!," he said, emphatically! "I see, I see. Ok."

"I will fax you our itinerary so you can get it to your people who are picking us up in Amsterdam . I made a mental note to let Dr. Bern know that we would need security personnel on the private flight from Amsterdam to Iran. There must be a general aviation section in Amsterdam. Security would have to meet us there."

There was a constant stream of foot traffic running by ouer bench. I was just people watching when I saw Mr. Grey suit about 4 people back.

"Wait a minute, Bobby." when he got close, I stood up, reached in my coat pocket , pulled out a hankie. I walked three steps to intercept him and said, offering him my hankie, "Sir, here is my handkerchief. It has my scent on it for the bloodhounds."

He took a step back and said, "Oh, Oh." His shoulders shrugged, eyes fell; ashamed, he took the hanky and walked away. "You' all better watch out what you're getting into!" he shouted back over his shoulder.

"Who was that?"Bobby asked.

"That's the grey suit back at my condo."

"Really, man?" It took a minute to sink in. "How did......." He didn't know what to say. "We are being listened to. Gott'a be."

"Watch who you talk to."

The two surveillance techs on the roof across the street with the long distance mic had seen and heard my exchange with Mr. Grey suit and were still laughing. Now I was scanning the rooftops and skyline for any indication of surveillance, but I didn't see anything. I took out a notepad and wrote *3:00, Friday, Delta, Flight No. 643 to Amsterdam. Dulles International. Bring all we talked about.*

I handed the note to Bobby. He read it carefully. Still, wide-eyed, he nodded his head in agreement. I shook his hand and stood to leave. "Keep quiet. Don't even use the phone, if you can help it. Not even your mother."

"See, ya here" and I pointed to the Dulles Airport word. "

Ok, man," he said.

I walked away, toward the subway entrance.

I departed the Metro station and hailed a cab. "Willard," I said.

"Yes sir." came the reply.

My car was still in the general parking lot. I walked up to it, opened it and popped the hood. I looked carefully inside the engine compartment. No loose wires or fingerprints on the dust. I bent down and looked for any sign of apparatus under the car as far as I could see, but this sucker was low. On my way out of town the first stop would be a service station with a lift.

I was pretty sure it would not blow up but I wanted to check for tracking devises. I had a 'Low Jack' installed but I knew where it was located. I pulled the car up under the rain portico. A young strapping kid came out of the Hotel door. "Hey guy, two things, will you go up to 214 and get my suitcase? It's closed up and lying on the bed. Then come down a load my bag in this car, while I go to the front desk and check out. I need eyes on the car at all times. I handed him two twenty's.

"Yes sir" with a big smile.

I handed him my room key. "Two, where is the nearest service station where there is a lift?"

"Ah, that would be three blocks down Pennsylvania, on the right side. The old Exxon."

"Ok, great, I'll wait for you." I said. Off he went, taking a second look at the two twenty's before shoving them in his pocket. "Nice car, sir" as he went through the door.

In 12 minutes he had the bag in his hand and was coming back through the door. "Here it is, sir" as he put it in the back luggage area.

"Ok, now wait here while I check out. Nobody near the car."

"Yes sir" As I was walking in, he said kind as an afterthought, "Oh, it wasn't closed up."

"What's that?"

"It wasn't closed up. The suitcase—I hope I got everything. I checked the bathroom."

Now I was beginning to get mad. I knew I had closed it up before leaving the room for the Mall. Someone had rifled through it.

"Sorry," I said, "was it a mess?"

"Oh no sir, just a little".

"You're a champ. Thanks a lot, be right back." I went to the desk and paid my bill. The desk clerk looked at me a little funny, which caused me to turn slowly around and look behind me. There was the other guy at the breakfast table, this morning.

Taking my receipt, I turned and said, "Sir, I already donated."

He looked at me like I was crazy and he was a

stranger.

"Yes sir, I already gave a handkerchief to your partner walking out on the Mall to wave under the bloodhounds' noses. You look a little uncomfortable, ought to unbutton your jacket. Those biscuits will puff you up like a blow fish." I knew he had a side arm and couldn't unbutton his jacket. I slapped my hip in mock recognition of the weapon. "You all take care now." I turned and walked away. Got in my 'Vette and purposely squealed my tires loudly, for his sake.

I loved screwing with the Fed's. I had played their game the last time, back 10 years ago. They were so full of themselves. I didn't like their game this time. I didn't fully understand it yet.

I got down to Exxon, gassed up for the three-hour ride back, and asked to use their lift. Another $20.00.

"Sure.' There was one open. "Watcha' looking for?"

"I'm not sure but I'll know it if I see it." We raised the car up. I scrutinized the undercarriage but I couldn't find anything.

"Looking for a tracker?" he asked.

Was it that obvious?

"They don't put 'em under the car anymore." He walked around and behind my license tag he jerked something and held it up for me to see. There were two brass wires hanging from a small, black button. "This ain't no Lo Jack!"

"Thanks," I said and handed another $10.00.

"No problem, I don't know nothing. Nice car."
"Thanks", I nodded as I got in and sped off.

OK, well it's not like they don't know where I
live and I was going straight home. I just wanted to
screw with them a little.

Still, my anger was showing up in my gas pedal.
It was so easy to speed in this car. I determined to
use the cruise control and set it one mile under. Enjoy the ride. Watch the rear view mirror.

I used the time to think of all that could go
wrong with this adventure. It was scary when you
thought about it. About 60 miles in, I decided to
take another route on secondary roads. No inter-
states. There were a couple of town. A bar or two I
used to haunt. Man, I could use a drink.

I told Seri to call Border Jumpers while I drove.
"Hello, Border Jumpers…"

"Cindy," I interrupted her. "Mike Charles. Can
you have those two tickets, one way to Amsterdam
at the ticket counter at Dulles, Flight 643 at 3:00
on Friday?"

"Checking… yes there are two available."

"Good! Opposing aisles, if you can get them.
Yes, use my card on file."

Ok, that's done. Go home!

Except for that little pause for a Jack. Always did Jack and water when I was nervous. Nautical Bill's neon lights were still on, so I pulled in his lot. I hadn't been to Bill's in some time. It was a sort of country, wood frame building with a wooden porch and overhang. A few rockers, outside. Weathered. It looked like it had degenerated into a bit of a knife and gun club, if you know what I mean. A rougher crowd, couple of bikers, leather's, etc.

Pool table inside, music blaring. This was no place to relax! Well, I was here so I was going to have just one anyway. The bar was right inside the door so I bellied up and asked for a Jack and water. Served up, oh that was good. These days, it didn't take long for those spirits to circulate through my bloodstream. Used to be, I could drink Jack until the bottle was half empty before I could feel it. No more. Buzz was right away and two was my limit.

*Well,* I thought, *what an eventful day.* I felt I had Bobby straightened away for our flight. I had it arranged. We just needed to show up at the airport on time. Go home and lay on the beach for a couple of days. Why not?

Two bikers came in and were rowdy. I guessed about '3 sheets to the wind', they were still in the loud, happy stage and not mean yet. Hey, hey! I raised my glass in celebration to some utterance.

The guy slapped me on the back. I came to the con-
clusion that things could only deteriorate from here
on so I put a ten on the bar and headed for the
door.

"Hey! Where ya' going?" yelled my new buddy.
I knew I was in for the pleading treatment.

"Aw man! We need you, let's shoot some pool!"

"My stick is at the Jewelers," I shot back.

He looked at me funny, "At the jewelers?" he
said.

"Yeah, one of the diamonds fell out last week."

"Diamonds, whoa!, I don't want to play against
you."

"I gott'a go anyway. Have to meet my probation
officer at 8." Tattooed biker's could usually relate to
that need, and this guy was a walking art gallery.
"Can't be late!?

"Yeah, man, I know about that!"

I knew I had naturalized the foray when I heard
that.

"Hey man, what's yours for?" he wanted to
compare infractions, kind of a one-up man ship attempt.

"Felonias Mopery," I added, knowing this was
an old English law prohibiting disrobing in front of
a mule.

"Oh, yeah," not knowing what to say.

I took quick advantage and made my way
through the door and out to my car. *Whew! Ok*

*Mike let's get down the road,* I thought.

Glad to be on my way, I found myself having visions of what might happen to this guy on his two wheels on his way home in his mental state. Maybe if he got a little drunker, his buddies wouldn't let him ride it. I cleared second gear and put it behind me. I could catch a night cap at the Sandpiper, back home on the beach one block from my condo.

Down the final leg of the beach highway and I was there. No, I am just going upstairs and chill in my floating living room. The elevator door opened to my floor and I stepped out almost bumping into the young, blond lady, Jennifer, I had met a few days before. "How ya' doing?" as I passed by, acknowledging our previous encounter.

"Oh, good! Having a great time."

"Thought you were up on 10," I said.

"Isn't this 10?"

"No, 8."

"Oh, my God!" She exclaimed, "I got off on the wrong floor! Too much gin!" Giggling, and turning back towards the elevator.

"Hey, it happens," I said back. The last thing I wanted tonight was a tipsy woman on my hands. Besides, I was much older than she.

I unlocked my door and went inside. At first, everything seemed in place, I wasn't expecting it not to be. Then I noticed the table at the end of the couch with the small, thin drawer, slightly ajar. Not alarming in itself, but back in my office where my computer was there were signs of disturbance. There were pages standing slightly out of one of my files, just a little. The average person might not notice but I was anal about my files. Couldn't stand a mess. Stacked and squared. It was my German heritage. Someone had been in here. But, still, I couldn't be certain. I just filed it away mentally, reflecting back on the events of this morning.

I looked, carefully for any signs of a bug. Even removed the air conditioning return grid. Under the desk, etc. I did not see anything obvious. Finally, I marked it off to an overactive imagination and made ready to go to bed. A hot shower after the long drive felt good. A Tia Maria on the rocks settled my latent tensions. The last thing I remember is one of those mega speedboats, a cigarette style, screaming up the channel, twin 454's making all the power they could, which meant the boat was going way too fast for conditions and the narrow channel. Just out of the bar up the street, no doubt. I knew my boat, in the slip downstairs would be rock' in and a rolling! But I had it secured with special expanding lines for that reason.

The sun hit my bed early on Wednesday. With the glass panels rising from the floor, and the height of the bed, your line-of-sight could not see the floor. You were looking down at the water and the bulk-headed channel, the city rising just eight stories below. There was a concrete deck, an extension of the floor which wrapped completely around the unit, with a railing, of course. A great place for morning coffee on my small, round, wrought-iron table. The smell of salt air and the town getting busy for the day was energizing. *Good morning, Lord!* I had always had a strong faith and sense of a spiritual presence moving with me through time and motion. Just talked to it all the time.

*Well, time to get rolling. I'll just put on my bathing suit and go downstairs right to the beach and take a walk. Great shells, this early. No, I better call Dr. Bern. His day will be half over by now.* "Yes, Dr. Bern," I said when he answered. "We are taking Delta Flight no. 643, Departing Dulles to Amsterdam at 3:00 PM. It arrives at. 1:00 AM. We will need two of the security team on board our private jet provided by the Iranian contingent. Pilot doors will be locked and we will be the only ones on the plane. They may have one attendant. These two can then wait for the rest of the team at our pickup location. I'll let you know where."

"Ok, Michael, and how are you doing?"

"Well, we've been careful but I have detected some surveillances over here. They listen to everything these days, you know!"

"Yes, I know, be very careful, Michael," he warned. "Once you are here, you vile have the very best team in Europe to protect you."

"Thank you, sir, I'll count on it."

"Call me anytime on this direct number," and he gave me his ultra-private, direct number.

"Thank you again, Dr. Bern. I am looking forward to seeing you again."

No one was up yet. I slipped down the elevator unnoticed in a white terry beach wrap and beach walking shoes. The nylon kind you could get wet. Very peaceful. Just a few folks farther up the beach, looking for shells.

Thursday was attorney day. I stopped by his office to double check on my will and make more provision for my grandchildren. If I didn't make it my estate would still be paid any proceeds of the venture. Same for Bobby. I went to the shopping mall and bought a few needed items.

Soon it was Friday morning. I had to leave at 5 AM to get to Dulles International, pick up tickets, meet Bobby and allow time for all the security crap since 9-11. I did have a membership in the Red Door Club, so the wait was endurable and productive. A nice lounge was provided for members, snacks, just about anything. They could pre-board you from the club.

I took the 'Vette again and hit the interstate to DC. I turned on the radio. There was a program all about how extensive was the 'Listening Network' in the USA by the NSA. Of course, all in the name of Terrorist protection and National Security. A recent leak by a whistle blower had spilled the beans and officials were not happy about having to explain the allegations. They really wanted to hang this guy for high treason. He had to flee the country.

Well, turns out the net is far and wide. Words are purged for analysis from every source. Computer, Cell phone, land line. Phone on or off, you could be heard in general conservation and tracked! *Ah Ha!* I thought. *That explains a lot to me.* I checked my rearview mirror. I got off at the next exit, to get back on again, checking for any followers. *Was I being slick or just paranoid?* Then I had the thought that surveillance could be done from way above silently. Not the old fashioned method of following in a car unless you were in the city. No joy that I could tell.

Back on the North-bound side of the interstate now, my nervous energy came out in my right foot. I hit that baby and it slapped me back in the seat and treated me to some G's! Man, this new 'Vette was fast! Problem was I knew I couldn't out run a radio. Again, I decided discretion was the better of valor and settled down to the speed limit. I mean, this car was RED! *Fool. Jealously and all that, they would love to put your ass under the jail!* A quick 130 mph! Oops! I can hear it now. "Well no, officer, it was the music! My foot was keeping time with the tune of 'California Sun" sorry, I got into the high B flat! Then tell him that your driver's license was in your trunk. Offer to get it. It's in your fishing box. Now we talk of fishing lures. Bass and fishing stories, exchanged. We were buddies then, as a fishing friend, I would never get a ticket. Just some good advice on lures. Used to work every time, but now - who knows ? I didn't want to find out.

I call ahead to Bobby to make sure he was up and active and to tell him to meet me at Delta ticket counter. Early. We would go to the Red Door Lounge Area from there.

"OK. Man, I will be there. How are you doing?"

"Doing OK, but be careful what you say over the phone or to anybody. I think we are being watched."

"Really?" in disbelief.

I reflected on Bobby's naïveté. "Do you watch the news? It's all around us."

"I ah will be dare". And we hung up.

In DC, I had to cross town, get to the GW Parkway and head up to 495 Beltway and out Rt. 66 to the Dulles Access Road. Things had changed so much. I remember the Dulles Access Road when that is all that it went to: straight out to Dulles and back. Uncle Frank used to let my drive his Jag 120, egg-shell white, red leather interior, when I was under 16 and didn't have a license. It was 14 miles of straight interstate. No access, straight to Dulles and back. Was I cool or what? Now there was an entire city out there. Herndon had grown. I had an inner Interstate leading only to the Airport, now.

Thing about DC is that it is always growing. My brother in-law is a builder and did interior build-outs there for new business. Of course, elections would change the faces, stimulate the start-ups, add Beltway Bandits—as we used to call them; any-thing to stay close to the 530 'Talking Heads' that came to town once in a while, if they could work it around their vacation schedule. I mean, talk about Hustlers! Made you wonder why it cost so much just to say Yea or Nay. And hammer a gavel down. I grew up in this city. I ran in the government build-ings since 1949. I had seen unimaginable growth since then and the family had benefited from the burgeoning Real Estate Market, up grading to ever larger homes and moving into the suburbs. The Megalopolis grew until the East Coast encompassed Baltimore, Washington and Northern Virginia in one big area. Remembered the two-lane country roads. Needed to connect these areas, from the late 60's. The Red barns and rural white ranch fences corralling Maryland Race horses were a thing of the past. Up came my exit. It was time to stop reminiscing. So much for nostalgia. But this area had so much to offer.

I peeled off and onto the ramp. This 'Vette was so smooth in its distribution of power. I had owned a Honda CBX, six cylinder Café racer in '79. It was billed as the fastest accelerating production motor vehicle made in the world with a 0 to 60 time of 3 ½ seconds, same a as a Ferrari today. But you were on two wheels. Six carbs. Six exhaust. 11.5 to 1 compression ratio and redlined at 10,000. It weighed 540 pounds, so I knew what raw power was. Pocono's to the Shenandoah Valley, down Skyline Drive in the Blue Ridge Mountains. In various vehicles, my airplane, My Mercedes Benz 450 Roadster.

Chapter 4

International Flight To The Middle East

Here I was, in the Dulles parking lot. Wasn't tailed, as far as I could tell. My luggage was light and I started to make my way to the concourse. Then, I thought, *Nobody will mess with us before we can get the bonds out of the safety deposit box in the bank. It wouldn't do them any good. The time to be really alert is afterwards.*

*Oh, damn,* I hadn't called Kali. *I'll call her from the lounge.*

Dulles was a truly unique airport. I had known it since its construction and first service. All glass and completely transparent, front to back, with immense , vertical arches the length of about two football fields wide. You could view out through the building to the busy tarmac. A unique piece of architecture for its time back in the early 60's. The city still had DC National, but mostly for domestic flights. The Jumbo's and transatlantic flights originated here at Dulles. You boarded into a large bus-like vehicle and were transported out over the tarmac to a secondary staging area, where the vehicle lifted high to the airplane door to allow access to the interior of the plane. However, I was headed for the "Red Door" lounge and club. I just had a Carry-on bag. My only anxiety was the ceramic Glock down by my ankle and an x ray machine. "I have a pace maker and an artificial heart pump usually got me to a 'shoes-off, wand-waving' security check. Too much liability fear had moved into panic after 9-11. Procedures were changed. Not eliminated. The ceramic was far enough up my leg to avoid a visual from shoe removal. Of course unloaded, in case some mitigation was needed.

I found the 'Red Door Club' and went in. I presented my itinerary and membership card to the attendant and told him that I was two hours early from flight time. I asked him to have a runner retrieve my and Bobby's tickets as we would wait to board when called.

"Yes sir, right away," he said as he checked his computer against my membership number and picture I.D.

I sat down, ordered a drink and called Bobby. "Hello, are you close?" was all I was willing to say. "Coming into parking lot now," came the response. "Good! Meet me at the Red Door Club, inside just down from the gift shop."

"Ya, Ok, man. See you in a few minutes".

I dialed up my daughter, Kali.

"Hello, dad," she came on. Ah! The wonders of caller ID. "What are you up to?"

"Well, I am out at Dulles Airport getting ready to leave for Iran, and I wanted to touch base with you first."

"Um hum.".

"Honey , I stopped by Attorney Nymark's office and updated everything, also Bobby and I have a pact for the dispersal of proceeds to you kids , in the event something goes terribly wrong. But it won't," I added quickly.

"Um hum, Dad, you know how I feel about this trip. I don't like it at all!"

"I know, honey, but we have arranged to have a world-class security team accompany us at all critical times of exposure. "I feel comfortable or I wouldn't be going."

"Yeah sure, Dad. If you stayed here both you and I would be comfortable."

"Just say a prayer for my safe travel and I'll be back before you know it."

"I'll be gritting my teeth all the way. Well, I am glad you called. You take special care and keep us and all the grandchildren in mind before you go out on some limb. I Love you, Dad."

"I love you all too, honey, don't worry.

About that time the door opened and Bobby peeked around the corner, not sure he was in the right place. He spotted me and his eyebrows raised up in recognition. I motioned for him to occupy the leather chair next to me.

"How was your trip over here?"

"No problem, man," he said. "I am ready to go. Where are the tickets?"

"I've sent for them. They are waiting at the ticket counter. They'll be here in a minute." Are your people meeting us with the plane as agreed in Amsterdam at arrival, that's about 1 am."

"I called with the Itinerary you faxed me, they said no problem. We will have to get to the General aviation side of the airport, by a cab."

"Ok, good work," I said. "And so, Bobby, how are you feeling about this journey and adventure we are about to embark on? Do you have everything you need?"

"I feel good. A little scared because of the people we are dealing with and some of the things that have happened since we began. I had no idea there was such a wide net listening to communications."

"Well, that depends on what they are hearing as to what they will pursue further. We are involving parties with policies and activities, not just ideologies, which are antithetical to our own. In addition there is a heck of a lot of money involved.

-

When the money hits the table, all the greed shows up, rationalizations begin, born of imaginations of why this is mine. It's human nature.

"Look what happens when treasure is found on a sunken ship in territorial waters. That country lays claim to it. Doesn't matter who found it or how much money they invested to retrieve it. Maybe some pirate, or some war, caused it to be where it is, even ocean currents, 200 years ago, but 'That's ours' prevails. And the 'Ours' will be a select few.

"Now, various entities can lay some kind of claim to what we are going after. The US for retrieving you uncle, the government of Iran, because the money was from the people. They'll want to nationalize it. Israel will not want it used against their people. Germany would like to get those serial numbers and decay those bonds because they don't want to have to redeem them, neither the US backing."

"Yes, I see the danger but I can't just leave them where they are."

"I know. And hence, our adventure commences. Oh, incidentally I've modified my will to include my share to my children if anything happens to me over there. My attorney is Bill Nymark, where I live. He will know what to do if it is necessary to contact him. How about you? Write down who I should contact for you now. I'll put it in my wallet."

"Yeah, ok, good. he started to scribble in a napkin and gave it to me.

"Well, stay sharp, beware, and hopefully this will go smooth. I think I've got the bases covered pretty good. My Daughter Kali is still upset that I am going."

I took another sip of my drink and in came the concierge with our tickets and a luggage cart. Time to go!

It was not with just a little apprehension that I stood up, as did Bobby by my side. We looked at each other with a mutual stare of understanding of what we were about to do so far away.

We followed the concierge out the door and down the short hall to the open airport, bright and sunny. It was a busy sight, with people everywhere. Planes in the distance way out about ½ mile out docking, loading, coming and going. The pace picked up. We were led to our boarding area for our huge, strange bus. We presented out tickets to the ticket attendant who promptly processed them. She paused, watching her screen, she picked up another telephone on her desk and announced some sort of code into the receiver. At the same time , she politely asked if we would mind standing aside for just a moment, motioning only a short distance to her right.

*Here we go*, I thought. In about 15 seconds, there appeared two gentlemen in airport security uniforms who very politely explained that this was a routine, random screening for parties traveling to 'Certain' locations, as part of our National Security Mandate. "Could we see your passports and any other paperwork you may have, please?"

We all moved to the end cap of the ticket counter for a place to lay out our documents.

The senior officer was looking intently at the documents and itinerary and mumbling under his breath. I heard, "Iran, Tehran, returning date?"

" Oh we are traveling by private jet, on to Switzerland and returning here in several days."

"We want to do some skiing," I added, afraid Bobby was about to get us into trouble.

He looked up and said "Short time for such a long trip?"

Bobby spoke up and said Yes sir , I am Reza Pahlavi's nephew, you know, the Former Shah, and I am just going to bring back some family items, sir. It will only take a short time. We really don't want to hang out over there. We have to go while we still can, if you know what I mean."

He looked pretty intently into Bobby's eyes and said, "Yes, I believe I do, Mr. King." He had never addressed us by name up until then.

He stacked the papers together and said, "Everything seems to be in order. You gentlemen have a safe trip today."

I breathed a sigh of relief. I didn't see the colonel from the Pentagon standing behind the column, the one who wanted tanks off balance sheet, trying to get a good look at us. Fidgeting, how was he going to pull this off? Rubbing his hands together. Turns out the colonel was behind this brief inspection, so he might have a closer look at us.

*Whew,* I thought as we were ushered back into the boarding line for the taxi bus vehicle. I was pretty sure no one was going to stop us before we had the bearer bonds in hand.

It was about a 12 minute ride out to the airplane boarding area.

"What was that all about?" Bobby asked.

"Oh, just routine," I said. I didn't want to worry Bobby into frenzy. He was a high spirited kind of guy anyway. "Well, we are on our way now." I said.

Feeling down my leg to see if my ceramic was still there. Amazing how that worked. Of course, I unloaded it for airplane travel. It would enhance my excuse if it were discovered

Into the transport bus and soon we would be in the air, heading for Amsterdam. I've heard so much about it. Exiting!

The bus lumbered along at a snail's pace to the Jumbo 747 we were about to board. The bus actually pulls up to the airplane side door and a long gangplank apparatus is extended into the airplane. It came to a halt. We grabbed our bags and stood up. We followed the crowd and walked onto the airplane.

"We have 4D and 4E, they should be on opposite sides of the aisle for easy access. It's a long flight, you know," I said. "Here we are; which side do you want?"

"Right here," Bobby sat down on the inside end seat and that left me with the outside end. We were close to the bar/lounge upstairs and the restrooms. "Hey! After takeoff, let's go up to the lounge and play some Gin." We used to play heavily in the office back in the 80's, while waiting for customers. A favorite pastime that had a way of eating up hours. "Ok, Hollywood, knock with the down card, penny a point?" Bobby said.

"Sounds good to me". I confirmed.

We squirmed around and got settled in before the attendant came forward for the taxi, pre-flight demonstration. There was a moment of silence as we waited.

Bobby began, "Hey Man, I really want to thank you for helping me with this. I know it has taken a lot of thought and preparation and now we are ready to go. Thanks again, Michael. Whatever happens," he reached to shake my hand.

"Hey, man," I said. "I am happy to be a part of this adventure! We are going to make out fine. We will actually be a part of history, with your uncles' legacy. And we will be rich, eh? No, it is I who thank you, Bobby. We have met again after these years, by providence! I think it is because of this that we will not fail. Put it in the hands of the Mighty One."

"Ya, Ya oh Yeah." Bobby most enthusiastically agreed.

Here came the flight attendant now. "May I have your attention, please?"

We were being pulled out of the gate, slowly, silently. Then came the low wine of the big GE jet engines, warming up. The flight attendant finished up her demo. It was a long ride to taxi out to the runway. Finally we turned onto 25 R and began a takeoff roll and then rotation and DC became a small panorama out the window. This would be a long flight.

"Yes ma'am, a Jack and water, please. We will be going upstairs to the lounge for a card game as soon as we can unbuckle. We used to fly the 707's with the card table up front on the right."

"Wow, that was a while ago"!

"Yeah the 70's," I added.

As soon as the seat belt sign was extinguished, we headed for the upstairs lounge. We seated ourselves at the card table and asked for a deck of cards. After stripping the deck, I prepared a sheet of paper in three columns' for Hollywood where you play three overlapping games at once. With a high down card, I always moved to 'Knock' as soon as I could get under it. "Yes, please, another Jack," to the attendant upstairs.

The flight was long and dark over the ocean. We were about even in the Gin game, money-wise. It was getting a little boring now. I said I wanted to go back downstairs and catch a little shut eye. I wanted to be sharp for arrival and our task at hand. Bobby agreed and we both went to our seats. The hum of the jet engines and the few drinks we had was enough to put us both into a deep sleep.

I awoke to an announcement about being 20 miles out from Amsterdam International Airport, and an attendant offering coffee. "Yes, two, please;" and I shook Bobby's shoulder. "Hey, man, time for a coffee. We are practically there."

Our approach, landing and taxi was normal. It was a little cooler than back home. We walked through the gate, wide-eyed. There was a man, looking like a pilot, holding a placard up written in Farsi.

I did not recognize it, but Bobby pulled me aside and said, "Over here."

We went aside and Bobby began to speak with the man, shaking hands. I stepped up also.

Bobby said, "He has a cab outside to take us to

the plane they sent. It's around the other side of the building, about 10 minutes."

I had spoken to Colonel Reeder about meeting us here at 1 pm. I did a 360, looking carefully. I saw a Green Beret kinda guy walking towards me.

"Oh, I think this is our advance security detail, Bobby."

"Mr. Charles?" he held out his hand. *Wow what a vice grip!* "I am Col. Reeder. We spoke."

I nodded and said "We have a cab outside to take us to the general aviation terminal."

"OK well, we've got our bags. Let's go."

Reeder fell into step behind the three of us. Bobby turned around and shook his hand.

We passed through the doors to the cab waiting at the curb. It was late so there was diminished activity. The pilot spoke to the driver directing him around to the general aviation terminal.

We pulled up to the open door of a black—yes black—Saber liner jet. It had a high overhead. You could walk around inside. These were very nice in their day about 25 years ago but not very fuel efficient these days. *Who cares when you have a lot of oil, I guess.*

True to the instructions, there was only a pilot and copilot and they left the cockpit door open for us to see that there was no one other on the plane , save a short , female attendant, who asked us I we would care for any refreshments. And then they closed and locked the bulkhead door as the attendant passed what looked like two coffees into to them.

Bobby said, "Yes, we will have the coffee too, please." He looked at Col. Reeder for acknowledgement.

Soon the Saber Liner was spinning up its engines. The captain announced, in English, that the weather was good tonight all the way into Karaj. The tension abated as we taxied to the runway. We got clearance from the tower and were soon on a takeoff roll. Up we went into the night.

The attendant brought us our coffee as we leveled off. I am guessing 25,000 feet. I leaned over to Bobby and asked him if he knew anything about the people we were going to meet.

"Just one", he said. "He contacted me about 3 months ago with a proposal. I don't really know how he knew I had been left these instruments by my uncle. Maybe the barrister that prepared the documents. Reza is dead and after theses years , there's no telling where loyalties lie. I m afraid I don't know much about him."

All of a sudden it hit me and gave me an uneasy feeling in my stomach. We were traveling at 4-500 miles per hour through the dark of night in and over a foreign land to a destination I had no frame of reference for, in a hostile land to meet a complete stranger who coveted our Gold Bonds. I felt no grounding. I was not accustomed to being at the mercy of others. I got up and went to Col. Reeder's side and sat next to him.

"Any advice, Colonel?" I asked.

"Just be sharp. Expect anything and be prepared for a quick exit. As soon as we land , I will send coordinates to the rest of my team to meet me at the airport with our own, specially equipped Lear 75. We will be ready for a quick extraction directly to Dr. Bern in Switzerland. Once the bonds are safely in his vault, we can relax and not before then. We will be ready for any adverse action until then, Mr. Charles."

Soon, we were descending and then on approach to land. We touched down on the runway in a dimly-lit facility. We taxied to a barely-lit metal building behind the air port terminal, if you could call it that. The jet engines began to wind down as we parked at the opening of the metal building. Actually a hanger, now that we were closer.

I heard a voice outside. Soon a key turned in the door hatch lock and the door opened. Since Bobby knew the language, I motioned for him to exit down the hatch stairway. I didn't know what or who was out there. I heard him speaking and being right on his heels, I soon saw a small, young man who was shaking hands, welcoming, and grinning from ear to ear. I remembered that these people were known for their hospitality, for centuries. This was somewhat settling to me.

Col. Reeder was right behind me and seemed to know his way around the protocols. Bobby was doing just fine with the young man. The pilots which were sequestered in the cockpit now came out with their pilot luggage. Flight cases.

# Chapter 5

## The Nehalem, A Mystery Man

They deplaned and said, "We hope you enjoyed your flight, gentlemen," and walked directly into the hanger.

"Yes, thank you," we called after them.

The young man said a car would be here any minute to provide transportation for us . Col. Reeder interjected that he would be staying here at the airport facility waiting for our ride back to arrive.

"There is a lounge inside. You will be comfortable, sir." said the young man, pointing in the direction of the terminal.

"Good, I'll get a coffee"

The colonel pulled me aside and gave me two phones. "These are secure and only have my number in them. You two use them to contact me until we meet again."

"Ok, great!" I said and took them.

Just then a long, black, Mercedes limousine pulled into our area.

"Ah," said the young man. "Your ride is here."

The driver got out and opened the rear door for

us and we got in. There was daylight on the horizon and we could see our surroundings much better.

"I think this airport could use a little remodeling," Bobby said.

"It was the closest General Aviation airport to our destination," I said. "But this limo sure is nice. I've only seen these in the movies," as my hands caressed the fine leather and opened the Burl Wood Bar doors with curiosity.

The driver got in. "Are you comfortable? We are only about 20 minutes away from our destination."

We both said "Good" at the same time. And off he drove to the airport exit and on to a nicely paved highway.

Finally, we could see hills in the distance and the driver pointed, indicating that was where we were going. After five miles or so, we turned off onto a side road which wound off around some hills. There was plenty of green vegetation now. Large fronds and long, wide leaves. It was rather like an oasis after riding through desert country. I could tell we were ascending to a higher level. My ears were popping. And the automobile engine was sounding the strain of an up-hill load.

Presently, we came into a cleared area with a wide paved circle and entry pillars to some sort of an estate. There were successive tin pillars every

100 feet or so, about 30 pillars in all.

"Where are we?" Bobby asked.

"Oh, this is a well-known place, sir. It is called 'The Pillars' by most people."

Bobby took note for a future call, in case we had to leave on our own by our own means.

"The Pillars", he repeated. "We are going right over there to that arch in the rock face. We will enter there and meet a guide to take us to your contact. Ok?"

"Sure," I said as I felt for my Glock. *Oh! I haven't loaded it. There is no ammo because of the commercial airline flight. Great!*

We parked and got out of the limousine. A guide appeared at the entrance of what could be described as a cavern. The walls were lined with dim lights every 25 feet or so. Just enough to see where you were stepping.

It was a dark shadowy cave-like structure for about 50 feet. Our guide was very quiet, circumspect of all around him, like he was expecting something to jump out at him. He spread his hands behind and outward indicating for us to stay behind him as he ventured forward and then after a right angle turn, the room opened into the light. A semi-brilliant light from all around. Sort of emanating from the walls. I couldn't tell. It was eerie.

There were small animals perched high on the rock on small pedestals. They were quiet and watchful. I thought I had seen them before but couldn't quite place where. Then, in a flash of recovery, I knew where I'd seen them. They were wide-eyed Gargoyles like I had seen on old buildings, high up near their or on their roof ledges. But these were alive! Amazing! They did not take their eyes off of us.

A very tall—maybe 10-12 feet tall—Turban-clad, dark-skin man came from around a corner and behind us. He was dressed in a deep purple, looked to be satin, drape. His pearlescent white turban literally glowed. It seemed to emanate light. He was possessed of a grand, white smile and greeted us warmly.

"Whoa, what a big guy," we both said at the same time.

"Greetings, my friends. It has been a long journey for you here. Please rest yourselves and accept some nourishment and refreshment," as he swept his very long right arm in the direction of three chairs—couches, really.

An attendant of normal size suddenly appeared with a tray of fruit and dates, nuts and small pieces of bread. "I trust you will enjoy these," he said with confidence.

We moved cautiously to the couches and sat down. It was like sitting on cool air. Actually, the whole room was cool. Air seemed to circulate easily by itself without any apparent machinery or sound.

He waited politely while we partook of the beautifully arranged items served on a bright gold tray.
"The beverage is a special , local juice blend from
our mountain fruit trees. I hope you will like it.
Very refreshing. The trees were cross pollinated
with the coca plant to give it a special quality for
enhancing your energy level. Just a little."

Finally, he began. "You may know me as
Shenaee Duma. I am descended from the ancient
Nehalem people, spoken of in your spiritual records. We are the progeny of the "Daughters of Men.
I must speak to you in your primal and circum-
scribed language so you will understand my dialog.
Our tongue is quite different than yours. I have
been permitted to disclose the following record to
you.

"Do not worry about taking notes. You will remember everything that is said in great detail,
much like your small transistor radio battery, say a
double A, will power a radio receiver for many
miles, effortlessly. And there is a gas component in
the atmosphere of this cave-like structure which
will enhance all of your senses."

In a very deep, baritone voice, he went on. "You
see, from ancient times your earth has been our
playground. We are descended from the Fallen
Ones, if you can accept that. Yours is an experimental world. There are many similar planets like

yours but far apart in the Great Space, which is always growing/expanding.

"Your Planet is approximately 4.5 billion years old—to date—and has benefited from many interventions of biologic up-lifting along the way. The ancient Annunaki visitors created an advanced civilization here to mine gold from the deposits in Southern Africa. Refined into a white powder, it became a fount of everlasting life. Heavy metals can have this beneficial effect. A so called 'Tree of Life', if you will.

"There was an admix of the Annunaki /Nehalem genetic material with your more primitive ancestors. This was hundreds of thousands of years ago. Your history fable, including the famed, Plato, makes reference to the Atlantian civilization; very advanced in science and technology. Making use of the technology of low frequency sound waves, they were able to erect many of the large monolithic structures still remaining today.

"This genetic material was diluted and remains somewhat flawed. It contained some psychological inconsistencies but the progeny was adequate for the task projected. Big and strong, well developed physical specimens with great endurance. The 'aberrations' were controlled by their masters. They were bread for intelligence and labor capacity, endurance.

"After the Atlantian collapse, through an unin-

tended over application of sound-moving technology, extreme vibrations undermined the very structure of multi layers of what you call the 'Teutonic
Plates', deep in the earth. A major earthquake ensued. Your present day Richter scale would mark it
at over 15. This prodigious movement caused a vast
layer of the planet, including Atlantis, to fall be-
neath the oceans, while other areas of land mass
rose to the surface. This nearly world-wide destruction and rearrangement scattered the six races geo-
graphically and admixed mankind.

"Geological up-lifts gave birth to mountain
ranges that were Weather barriers and impassable.
Some continents were isolated for many millennium. The unfortunate result was a retarded development cycle, throughout the known world. Communications between peoples were truncated or
eliminated. The seas were unmanageable and fear-
some.

"Our ancestors had rebelled against the strict
confines of His—The Almighty Creator—will. We
were granted the right to do so. Our ancestors
alighted on your Earth as it was inviting and pleas-
ing to our eyes. This seventh major universe was
within our power manifestation frequency as to allow us to manipulate the matter /density vibration
into forms of our choosing. You know very little of
the light-transmitted, power, in the full spectrum.

"For example; if all light wave energy were a

spectrum represented by the end joint of your index finger," he stretched his out, his was very long, "the light you are able to see and eventually utilize is about the size of a human hair. You see, matter is amenable to thought energy. Even the Master, Jesus, exemplified this when he said you could move this mountain and cast it into the sea if you had but a little faith focused on the task.

"Anyway, all was reasonably respectable, even with provision for our redemption back into fellowship with universal Goodness, UNTIL we saw the 'Daughters of Men' and found them FAIR.

"We could not resist the temptation to mate with these temporal beings. Their 'logic formation' capabilities were not complete and they were an easy conquest, as you might put it. We were sure we could help their development with our DNA (Deoxyribonucleic acid) and there was that special Human-ness to their personalities.

"Personality has survival value in the universe. It really is the only thing that ultimately survives." He intoned. "Perhaps the Master should have used two ribs instead of just one when creating them from the prototype, Adam and the Adamic strain of DNA." He chuckled, deeply.

"We never understood the overall design for mankind and when we inserted ourselves in this way into the creation scenario, you would have thought we were the worst of Evil creatures! We hadn't been trained in the discipline of Genome manifestation on the Mansion Worlds by the Melchelzdsdecks, (a teaching order of beings,) at that point in our sojourn here.

"Worst of all, we lost our connection with the universal stream of consciousness that permeates most of the universe. We were 'cut off' from this essential communication and energy dissemination We, after a while, were so entrapped in this matter/ energy / space and time, human paradigm, that we lost sight of any way out. We were deserted by our kind who left us to our own devises,

"Well, The Master had no sense of humor about altering the genetic code of these experimental world, creatures 4.5 billion years in His making—including the planet itself. The God of All, got, well, pissed off! To put it into your terms.

"We had many progeny with your fair maidens and some were manifested as 'Mid-way' creatures that could not be seen with your allotted light spectrum wavelength, unless granted you by them. Some are still here, today.

"Looking through time, as only the Master can do, there were unacceptable future permutations which would have mitigated the long , long, efforts consummated up until that time.

"Much later on, a creature from the Nodite Tribe, advanced in intellect at that time, was able to convince Eve of the "Adam and Eve" order of biologic up lifters sent by the Master, to short cut this long process being performed in the First Garden through a liaison between himself and the Eve creature. The so-called 'Apple' scenario. The permutations of the liaison were immediately noted; 'Who told you you were naked?' and the Garden experiment was abandoned and then the Garden was destroyed.

"This new paradigm/Helix was passed on to your race at that time through our latent DNA in the Nodite race, thereby polluting it, that is; in terms of His Plan developed from the beginning of your so-called time.

"The introduction of the Nodite's genetic material, proved to be catastrophic to the uplifting! A longer gestation period for Eve's off spring and delivery, and through much pain.

"Moreover it altered, in a cardinal way, the vibrations which were able to be utilized for overall work and effort for daily duties and commerce. Hence, 'There will be much pain in childbirth' and 'By the sweat of your brow shall you live,'" were recorded in your sacred records to indicate the seminal shift with this life changing action.

"Eventually, using matter malleability and the fact that you all are a two gas breathing beings, He decided on the use of water H2o, to adjust your outcome going forward. He, with prodigious power manipulations, caused the most Eastern ocean floor to rise.

"He caused the release of multi-layered atmospheric precipitation—held in place by His power manifestation—to deluge and obliterate the land masses. He thereby introduced a third chemical element, namely, H2O, water, that a human cannot tolerate if the water displaces the other gases .

"Of course your history records a cautionary, sort of an end around run, if you will, with the construction of that saving ARK he asked Noah to build, to countermand the water effect for a chosen few, and some animals.

"In Noah, there were no compromised DNA molecules. This genome was unspoiled by our adventures with the fair maidens of men, as your history in the book of Enoch records. There are also references in the Psalms about The Councils on High, with regard to these adventures, and Gilgamesh

"So, in this game of *'Time Retaliation'*, fence and spar, thrust and pare, we are retaliating with a threatened nuclear conflagration on Earth to, basically, as you would say, move our Knight in this Chess game.

"We will place 'The abomination which Causes desolation' on the famed Temple Mount. This abomination is to the God head an atomic disintegration. A split in the fabric of creation. Of wholeness and therefore, Truth. Hence - an Abomination!. A suitcase-size apparatus  will do. Splitting an atom the sub atomic unit of God created matter/ unity, which can only be truth, is an abomination to God. Unnatural and with horrendous consequences. If placed on the temple mount, it would annihilate Israel!

"He will not let this happen. The God of all Gods will re-enter this dimension to neutralize our action. Why Israel ? you may ask. Certain promises were made to this tribe long ago. And the God of all Gods always keeps His covenants. He must. They will be no value after the conflagration. There will be no more chosen people of God unless He intervenes in some way. Our study of time folding technology indicates He might. And so, we could possibly negotiate our release back into the greater universe. We really don't like it here.

"Do we make mischief? Oh, yes, gentleman, we make much mischief." His voice became surreal, deep, and kind of echoed. There was a steel glare in his eyes,

"Our fate has been sealed and we must have a cognitive reassurance of our very selves to survive in this Earth time lock. Our greatest fear is isolation. We would like to, once again, traverse this sector of the universe."

*Wow!* Bobby had to sit down. He was reeling, just now, understanding what he had gotten us into. He looked, desperately for a way out! This was too scary. Couldn't go home if this were to happen.

Bobby repeated, "Your conquest will be useless for many generations. Do you represent the Iranian government?"

"Yes, but oh, you misunderstand this." Shenaee Duma explained. "We do not want to occupy or retain this conquest and its resources. We just want to neutralize or reverse all the 'Progress' your race has made through His over-control for thousands of years!

"Sort of like, 'Ok, your move now'. He has a very forgiving nature and may just set us free! He's done it before. There is just so much you do not know."

"You see, possession of self, which is a falsehood, as self only, and therefore a lie, embroils the soul entity within a matter mass. A vibration frequency of no escape. It is like a vault, a jail and you are your own jailer until you find the key. When you divert your attention you release it from cognition and Personality prevails again. Did you not understand the example provided of nailing self to a useless, dead tree to be instructive?

"For those who understand and follow, this will unlock every cell and allow an escape from that state from which it is so easy for our kind and our ancestors to hold you captive here in the bowels of this sphere. You know, there is more inside than there is on the surface, do the math!

"We are retaliating with a nuclear conflagration on Earth to basically, as you would say, 'Touché'. And so, when we will place 'The abomination that Causes Desolation' on the famed Temple Mount, it is to the Godhead an atomic split in the fabric of creation. Hence - Desolation. Suitcase size will do.

"We have enlisted globalist interests who are committed to our cause with billions upon billions of dollars, who really don't know why they are so motivated. Very wealthy Pawns, indeed. You would recognize their names. You sometimes call them Illuminati. They think of themselves as Proto-genital and superior. A trap of their own making They are co-opted with Minions and Principalities, unbeknownst to themselves.

"Of course, you did not know about the double helix of peptides until the early 21st century. or no value after the conflagration. There will be no more chosen people of God unless He intervenes in some way. Our study of time warp technology folding in-dicated He might. And so, we might negotiate our release back into the greater universe."

I stood completely dumbfounded. I glanced over at Bobby to try and understand the enormity of this endeavor and if he, Bobby, was aware of this evil scenario we were being invited into.

He hunched his shoulders and spread his arms, exclaiming, "I don't know, I don't know. How will you use the land and its networks of commerce if you do this?" He looked to Shenaee for an answer.

"Understanding in an flash of comprehension that it was Amah drama do-little's insecurity, and a corresponding, reaction formation in the mind of self/ego enhancement, that facilitated it's acceptance in his abbreviated mind construct. It—his mind—allowed for a continuum of reality affirmation which made it easy for these beings to auto Cybernetticaly introduce this, their hoped-for epical conquest, into the reality these ideologists had created over millennium. Are you not one of these, Mr. King? You see, even Amadinadjad had been completely compromised by his own, obsessive focus. We simply use their human foible against them. It is NOT our construct."

Wow! Bobby had to sit down. He was reeling, just now, understanding what he had gotten us into. He looked, desperately for a way out! This was too scary. Couldn't go home if this were to happen.

Bobby repeated, "Your conquest will render these areas useless and barren for many generations." It was the only small part he could assimilate. Some of these trade routes along the Mediterranean Sea are from ancient times.

"Many of your ,so called, scriptural concepts are incomplete or flawed. This goes on through many millenniums. Now Mr. King's plan may help us bring this to another level."

Bobby showed his big, nervous smile now.

Shifting feet, he was very uneasy. "I, I, didn't know what this plan was!, Ah, I, ah don't know about ... Shenaee Duma cut him off with a glare. Steel like eyes, something was happening! The Gargoyle-like creatures lowered their heads slightly and there was a hissing sound. Shenaee Duma waved his hand and they retreated, shifting. "Ah, now, do not worry, my friend. You will be lying on the beach, say Monte Carlo or perhaps Australia? We are convinced He will intervene AT LAST, ANYWAY!"

We were both dumbfounded!

Arrangements had been made with the Bank, commitments that were not easily undone. What to do? Needed time to think. I could tell that Bobby was completely taken unaware. His face was ashen. He swallowed hard, sheer fear in his now shifty, white/black eyes.

I waved him over by my side, saying , "We have to talk. Would you pardon us for a moment?"

"Of course, take your time," came the reply, with a bowing gesture, His turban glowing now, again. "There are more refreshments in that room, through there."

Bobby grabbed my arm in desperation, pleading, "I don't understand half of what he is saying, man."

I knew oh so much better because of my scripture readings, life-long. I knew exactly what he meant. "Look, we must delay and get out of this cave for now. I don't want to piss this guy off, but he'll know what we are doing. We tell him we like the Monte Carlo destination and that we have to check on the Bonds, the Issue and our contact in Switzerland for blocking into a credit facility to get cash. Trust me, we gotta' get outt'a here! There are powerful forces at work here."

"Yeah man, I am scared."

"Yeah, me too. Follow my lead."

We walked back out into the main room, and seeing Mr. Duma, I said, "Mr. Duma, Sir," he was sitting and got up politely to address my concerns. "Yes, Mr. Charles, are you and Mr. King more settled now?"

"Well, to be frank and perfectly honest with you..."

"Of course," he said, offering a gesture of openness with his right arm. "Please feel free."

"Well, this is such an enormous plan with so many permeations to consider, we are frankly, quite taken aback by its scope and purpose." Feeling emboldened by my personal, religious belief system, I went on. "If you will permit me, sir, it seems to me that this self assertion and conquest is exactly what got you here in the first place.

He looked at me quizzically, tilting his head slightly.

"In other words, substituting your intention, born of your ego manifestation for the plan and will of the Creator Master.

"This biological uplifting process of the Adam and Eve Protocol, although lengthy, was in operation and working. That is, a breeding out of the Genome of certain personality traits which, when fully developed, lead to a concentration on self, being, and aggrandizement to the detriment of any objective evaluation of a circumstance and its status for the greater benefit of all parties to a specific act. In other words, Love, goodness and personality preservation, for a soul entity, as the primacy of the act. This violation was first noted by the Angel in the first Garden when the interrogative was declared, 'Who told you were Naked? when the first, primary order was compromised by The Nodite and the "Eve" prototype's modification to THE PLAN, conceived of, developed forward, and executed by The Ultimate Causation, The Holy Father of all. Holy means. 'Set Apart'.

"As thoughts are energy matter, this phase shift was not so much the physical manifestation to the eye gate of her physical nakedness but rather the blight of the knowledge of good and evil in the spirit.

"Possession of self reduces all vibration until matter becomes more dense and, falsely, life-like. While appearing to be alive , it is really dead or will die. The awareness of self, 'You shall surely die'. Both,wanting a covering, was a dead giveaway. Hence 'The Mother of the Living' as opposed to the undying. The Living die. The Living is a contrast mechanism to describe a new category of being.

"This, it seems to me sir, was born of attempt to 'up-lift' by another plan, as if it could be as sanguine as the Master's, all encompassing, multi faceted , inclusive in all respects, working out of the evolutionary construct for this realm and its endowment.

"Your aberration as 'Fallen Angels' fell into and became part of egocentricity infecting this construct. Now there ensued an embroilment in Matter, Space, Time and now, impotent energy. Indeed, 'By the sweat of your bow, will you labor' you just lost your inheritance, natural to the protocol. Ain't nothing goanna work the way it used to".

"This, actually was never your game, your sandbox. You were interlopers in this system, this quadrant, from the beginning . Your former 'advancement' emboldens you. You're going to get slapped down like a red-headed step child, Sir, and we humans will pay with our lives for your adventurous escapades! You're taking license with Eve and the out-working of The Plan has resulted in a embroilment in the flesh, a density which you can capture in MET—matter energy and time—you call it Hell, BUT, you see, He was forced by His love for the created being to come and 'Set the Captives Free'. By willfully, allowing and employing a crucifixion of this matter density—flesh—and overcoming your maximum limitation of our spirits, Death and everlasting entrapment here. He opened your confines that we would have life more abundantly! He freed, if you will, the matter density of flesh to be able to again expand to the former vibration frequency necessary to be released back into the universe. By employing belief, we make it possible to occur. You may contend for our souls at death but if we are in possession of the belief, the faith in the truth—Christ—we recognize His voice. 'My sheep hear my voice', and we belong to him and his vibration. Yours is defeated. Possession of the very belief is what makes it so. He already got your ass! Sir. He took His flesh, had it crucified for all of us and then overcame you petty limitations by His own power, returning to a morantia level of matter density and energy and making a way for us to follow Him, if we choose to in this new 'Glorified' body.

"You see, when we concentrate overmuch on an object or thing, we give it power over us, as you well know. Vibrations reduce and matter/density thereby ensues, trapping the focus entity.

"You are an awesome specimen, sir, and I don't wish to offend your sensibilities, but the high hill, the Temple Mount, many cities, kingdoms and gold will not work any better with Mr. King and myself then it did with the Master. We read the last chapter. I think you better fold your hand, beg for mercy! Knock off the mischief!, Sir. If you get outside of Time and observe, you will see that this has already been played out, and is sealed with the supreme, love act of the crucifixion and then the resurrection, back into life. Your opportunity may have passed you by, sir."

With a sad countenance, he began to tremble, barely perceptible, at first, then more pronounced. Then he started to shake, tremors were increasing! The Gargoyle-like creatures screeched briefly and evaporated! His physicality was reduced from his former austere bearing like a balloon deflating slightly. There was pain in his eyes. The turban was yellow and lost its former brilliance. His bluff had been called! There was no ace in the hole.

I felt a little sorry for Mr. Duma. I took a step or two over to his side and placed my hand on his shoulder gently. "A non-truth perpetuates matter density. Only pure truth provides the energy to escape it. 'I am the way, the truth and the life', He said. It really was a very simple message if you don't cover it up with matter sustaining, ego. In my country we would say 'Give it up , Dude'!"

He kept his head down but raised his eyes to mine, looking submissive, ashamed. "You are right, Mr. Charles, you both may go if you like. My assistant will guide you safely out."

Whew! , I was thankful for that! I thought Bobby and I were trapped in this lair. I could see the relief in Bobby's eyes. The assistant appeared out of nowhere, and beckoned us to follow him. "Don't mind the creature's noises along the way, They are now rendered harmless. Please, this way.

"Also, we have detected electronic surveillance focused on your person. Do you know you are being tracked, Sir?"

"No, I didn't. We will need a safe place for several hours, in that case."

The assistant said, "I believe this can be arranged".

"Do you have a secure telephone I can use?"

"Yes, right this way, sir." A small room. It appeared to be lined with sheets of lead.

"Hello, Dr. Bern?

"Hollo?"

"It's Michael, I need your help. Seems like I am being tracked by I don't know who. Our deal with our end user has crashed, tell you about it later. Right now, I need the security team deployed for an extraction from a small airport just outside Tehran. It's called Karaj Municipal Airport. We'll need a private jet, our team and we will have the bonds for you."

"Venn, Michael?"

I said, This afternoon!"

"Oh, my God, vat has happened?"

"Later. Ok?"

"Ok! You take care. I vill set it in motion"

"Tell security to say as little as possible when they call my number. No dates, No locations. Just ETA's We will be there. They can depart the plane armed but not obvious and ready for a protective extraction until we clear Iranian air space."

"Oooo, this is not gut, Michael."

"Yeah , I know, Heinz"

Bobby had witnessed all the foregoing and was white as a sheet.

"Do you have credentials for the safety deposit box, at the bank?" I asked.

"Yeah, gott'em here," he pointed to his inside coat pocket.

"Have a gun?"

"No, No gun."

"Ok, I brought my Glock; only two bullets between my toes. We will be vulnerable until we get to our plane."

"Let's go to plane first and get security detail before we go get the bonds."

"Good Idea, Bobby."

"Now, while I say goodbye to our guide, you step out the side, down that tunnel and get us a cab. We are going to Karaj Municipal Airport. Tell no one! I'll be right out."

"OK." Bobby was happy to get out of those environs. He ran for the exit. A cab was close at hand.

## Chapter 6

## The Stash-Security team

We told the security detail to standby and meet us in the coffee shop at Karaj airport. There were four of them. The lead guy was an ex special forces guy named Roger Albright. He was a formidable soldier. His team had performed with precision at Amsterdam and on to Karaj. Now we would have to locate them and move forward to the bank where the bonds had been held in a safety deposit box, since just before the Shah was exfiltrated from Iran by the U.S. team.

Little did we know that the U.S. Government had already envisioned a strategy to confiscate the bonds as a form of reparation payment for their aid to Reza for the extraction. General Bullock himself had put forth this idea to the State Department. He needed some Abrams Tanks and saw this as an opportunity to acquire them - *Off budget! Hot Dog!*

He had communicated this to the CIA with assets in the region. They had been tracking us since we had landed in Karaj.

"Sir, you have shown us tremendous kindness and hospitality and we are forever grateful. Is Mr. Duma all right."

"Oh yea, I think so," he made a circle with his finger around his right ear and rolled his eyes. I believe he thought of him as disturbed mentally. "You were very frank with him." he said as he grabbed my arm and walked me outside and opened the rear door of the cab.

He walked around to the driver's window and said something in Farsi. I thought indicating to go fast as he handed him a wad of cash, sweeping his arm forward. Looking inside for the last time, he winked again and handed, through the window a plastic box into my hand, which I reflexively accepted.

"It's secure!: It was a sealed box with a new phone in it. "Use this!" he thrust it at me. "You will hear others."

A business card was attached by rubber band to it. It read Agent Hillel, Mossad. "Now go quickly and be watchful. He slammed his hand on the roof of the cab over the driver's head, "Huddla, Huddla!"

Opening the side door, there was Bobby waiting. I had jumped into the back seat and said to the driver, "Karaj General Aviation Airport."

He stepped on the gas! I sat back and reached

for the cell phone that had been given to me. Looking at my old phone I retrieved Capitan Albright's number and called. All of a sudden, all the old numbers transferred just from a proximity to my old phone. *Neat,* I thought.

I remember hearing some advertisement for that feature. In fact, I had read recently that all the airwaves were, in effect, "Powered Up" by a proliferation of texting and there was now technology to appropriate it. All signals could be traced and tracked.

"Albright!" came the crisp answer.

"Captain, this is Mr. Charles, we have been tracked! No I don't see anybody yet. Our guide told us that they had picked up electronic surveillance. He gave me a secure phone and it turns out, he was Mossad!"

"Sounds like you guys have drawn some attention."

"Think so," I said. "Dr. Bern was afraid of this. We are en route to the airport to pick you and the team up before going to the bank to retrieve the bonds. We will feel much more comfortable with you guys around."

"Roger that," Mr. Charles."

"Our ETA , will be... just a minute, Driver, how far out are we?"

"Twenty minutes, this traffic," came the reply.

"Twenty minutes, Captain," I said. "Please be

alert for any development. Our deal with the Government rep. fell through. Long story, but they wanted us to finance their "Yellow Cake" production, intending to compromise the Dome of the Rock and annihilate Israel."

The cab driver stepped on the gas, noticeably, when he heard this.

"They might try to simply steal those bonds once we get them in hand!"

"Oh, shit! Roger that. sir," said the captain. "We will be on high alert. Come to the No. 6 hanger gate. We have a modified Lear 75, it will be at the ready."

"You said 'modified'?" I questioned.

"Yeah, very fast with a higher service ceiling . Also, anti-missile detection and a nose cannon. It will jump off the runway, Sir"

"We may need it"

What a dirty, dusty and noisy ride this was. The driver drove fast through patches of open desert and through narrow town alleyways. He was constantly checking his rearview mirror.

"Hey, watch out for that kid! We can't be stopped!" I screamed at his sliding.

I felt my ankle to see if my Glock was still there. It was ceramic and would avoid metal detection. A gift from Dr. Bern, several years back.

Then, I thought, *they won't want to alert us*

*before we are able to get the bonds in hand. Then watch out. Be on alert at the bank. May need some deception, misdirection.*

Bobby was hanging on for dear life.

"Have you ever seen the size of the package?" I yelled over the noise the cab was making.

"Once, when I came back a few years ago," he said.

"How large is it?" thinking ahead to some kind of concealment.

"Near as I can remember, about like this," he showed me with outstretched hands. "Wrapped in black paper."

"Great!" I said with astonishment. "We may need to disguise it to get it out the door of the bank. Neither one of us had any cover clothing on, none whatsoever.

*Have to think of something.*

We arrived at Karaj Airport. There was a guard at the gate to the General Aviation tarmac and staging area. We paused, "Hanger No. 6," I said. "Which way?" He pointed left around the corner and took another bite from his submarine sandwich. It was lunchtime, after all. A left turn, and we could see the captain, four men in fatigues and two uniformed pilots standing outside a dark grey Lear Jet 75. It seemed to have an exaggerated wing spar where it was attached the fuselage of the plane.

Same thing at the tail spar. The ailerons were thin, like titanium. It had appearance and characteristics of a fighter plane. He was waving us in.

The cab driver screeched to a halt just feet from the plane. Colonel Reeder barked out orders. "Pilots, stay here. Refuel and make the plane ready for quick departure. Johnson, stay with the plan. Harrison, Buell and Carter in the cab with me."

I jumped on Bobby's lap to make room. These were football-size guys. Colonel Reeder got in the passenger front. They all had small, concealed automatic weapons under their CPO Jackets, barely concealed. I reached my hand forward and said "Mike Charles, Nice to meet you. This is Mr. King under me."

"Colonel Reeder," he grabbed my hand firmly, nodded and replied, "Getting sticky, huh?"

"Could be. Can't tell yet. They won't show their hand before we come into possession of the bonds, I am sure."

"Got that right," he shot back.

I handed him the Card that was given to me from the assistant back at the cave. He took it and a broad smile followed with recognition of the name. "I know Hillel. Good man. Served with him at Entebbe years ago. Must be undercover here these days, or a double agent."

I thought I saw a slight smile cross the driver's lips.

"What about the weapons in the bank?" I said. "International security permit, by treaty. No Problem. We won't be flashing them around."

"Ok. Bobby, you know the way to the bank," I said assuming.

"Ah, ah, not far, It's in this town, maybe two blocks over, then left, I think."

"You think!" said Colonel Reeder. "This should have been scoped out in advance!"

"Yeah, I am sure. I checked it out on my GPS at home. I haven't been here in a while. Remember, I am the Shah's nephew. How do you say, Persona non Grata." He hit the driver on the shoulder for emphasis, "Two blocks down and left. Bank of Iran!."

"I know it," he said in a kind of a deep guttural accent.

"As close to the front door, as possible," I added.

He nodded his head. "Yes, sir!"

Now, the accent was strangely familiar but I couldn't place it. Then the hard drive mounted above my shoulders completed its search... *The Rabbi service!* I was a guest. "The Lord Your God is One God".....I could hear the accent. Was the cabbie Mossad, too?" I thought I detected some split second recognition in Colonel Reeder's face, as he glanced that way. Hearing what I did. Somehow, I felt better with our Jewish friends around.

We had arrived at the Bank front door. "Bobby, you ready? Got everything?" I said.

He nodded his head and Col. Reeder snapped an order. "Johnson, stay with the car but outside on the curb. Buell and Carter, both sides of the lobby. Mr. Charles, I'll stay close to you and Mr. King, OK, Go! Least time as possible inside! Cabby, wait here."

He had been well paid and just nodded his head affirmatively. We exited the car as inconspicuously as we could and stepped toward the doors. Inside, there were few people. There was a turban-clad gentleman in a chair in the corner and a much younger teenage youth, male, on the other side of the room. The youth was stout and had a soccer shirt on. The turban clad man was wearing a small blue dot , gold fraternal pin like the one I had seen on Mr. Duma. I took note for recall. It was not a terribly large front room. Our security took up positions as inconspicuously as they could as if everything were just pro-forma.

Bobby proceeded over to the teller counter with myself and Col. Reeder close behind.

"I need to see someone about my safety deposit box, please."

"Yes sir, right this way. Do you have your key and identification with you, sir?"

"Yes, I do, and I need to take this gentleman, Mr. James in with me."

"Yes sir, just one, please."

The colonel nodded and said "I'll be here at the entrance to the hallway, if that's alright?"

"He is a security officer," I added.

"All right," she said. "May I have your ID and see your key, sir?"

He used his original Iranian name.

The teller looked at the ID and was somewhat taken aback. She recognized the Pavli family name. "Oh, the ex-Shah's box. We were so much better off with him. Please, come this way. To the best of my recollection, this box has not been requested in years. It's paid for from a law office. Please follow me."

We proceeded down a hallway toward the safe. There was a janitor pushing his cart with a mop, a bucket and a large box of toilet paper on its top shelf. He moved to a side alcove where a door concealed his storage area. "

Oh, excuse me," he said as he opened the door to his area. And quickly moved from our path. A mental flash picture of his cart and supply room stayed with me. I was on high alert, I guess.

We proceeded into the safety deposit room and the teller walked over to a wall of drawers. She scanned and saw the correct number on her key. She stuck it in the box and said, "Mr. Bacthier, please insert your key under mine."

Bobby did so. She twisted hers to the right and asked Bobby to do the same. They both turned smoothly and the box jutted out slightly with a click sound.

"I will leave now, please take your time, sir." was her last remark, and she proceeded down the hallway.

"Ohm Miss?"

Sshe turned.

Can I speak with you?"

She walked back at my gesture. I was already formulating a plan of exit based on what I had seen already. "Do you have spare safety boxes stored?"

"Yes, we do." came the reply.

"Oh great, we will be taking this one out with us. Can you charge Mr. Bacthiers' account for one? We dare not expose its contents."

"Well, I guess I could…"

"Good, done!" I said, American style. I walked her down the hall and passed the janitor again, still fumbling with his cart. The toilet paper box was on the top tray still.

I reached out and jerked his shirtsleeve. When he looked back at me, I asked him if he spoke English.

"Yes," and nodded.

I reached in my pocket showed him a $100.00 bill and waved him back with me. He came willingly. I said "With the cart."

Bobby had slowly slid the box from its shelf and placed it on the table provided. He opened the lid ever so slowly, no doubt intimidated and awed by what was inside. There was a package, wrapped in black, waxed paper, folded and sealed. Bobby stepped back in awe.

"Ok, Bobby, I need one serial number for Dr. Bern to check out so he can justify these security expense advances. I will text it to him."

"Ok," he took hold of the package, the size of a Bond and about four inches thick and carefully peeled back the top fold, to reveal a bond in perfect condition. I quickly jotted down the number on my hand with a pen nearby. Bobby looked at me with question in his eyes when he saw me leading the janitor and his cart back into the room

"OK, listen. I didn't like what I saw when we came in the front door. We need a deception and misdirection. Now listen, you are going to take this box, with the flap closed and exit the bank." I reached for a paperweight on the file cabinet, grabbed a cleaning rag on the cart and quickly wrapped it around the paperweight.

"I don't think you will make it. If anyone challenges you or attempts to take it from you, resist them pull hard on this box and then finally let them have it. Go straight to the front door and hold it wide open. I will be running through it like a full back with this toilet paper box." I dumped it out and dumped the contents of the safety deposit box inside, careful to place 6 rolls of toilet paper on top.

"Now, sir," I turned to the janitor. "You walk your cart with the toilet paper box on top out into the lobby like everything was quite normal. Line it up 10 feet from the door very casually"—he was nodding his head—"and then take a rag and begin dusting the tables. Stay away from the cart. We will be several minutes behind you. Do you under-stand?

"Yes sir. I will do it."

"If I am right, all hell will break loose. Just stay out of my way as I come through," I said. "OK?"

"Yes, Yes!

He seemed to understand perfectly as he slowly walked his cart down the hallway and through to the lobby. His movements went rather unnoticed. Little did he know he was standing next to so much money. He paused about ten feet away from the front door and began to step aside, garbed a rag and began dusting the table blocking the sight path of the man in the Turban, who seemed agitated at the imposition. Our security team was on alert and this did not go unnoticed.

Handing Bobby the safety deposit box, I said "You're on. Now walk casually , showing the box, prominently. If someone grabs at it , struggle like it's your life. This will provide me the seconds I need to come from behind. Got it?"

"Yea, Yea, Good!"

"If not, nothing lost!"

"OK!"

Bobby went forward, showing the box. I walked three steps behind him. When he passed under the arch into the lobby, I noticed the feet planted firmly on Turban man, ready to spring and knew I had been right. All eyes were on the safety deposit box. I saw a nod from the Turban man to the kid soccer. Both of them on cue sprung for the box. Security reacted, pulling out their weapons, pointing them at these guys menacingly at these two. A shot was fired into the ceiling as a warning. This brought the bank security guard to the lobby with his gun drawn . The tellers were screaming and had dove to the floor.

Colonel Reeder shouted "Hold it. No one will get hurt!"

Carter and Buell stood at the ready, guns pointed. The bank guard recognized the futility of any resistance. Soccer kid and his obvious partner were attempting to grab the box from Bobby and yelling "This belongs to Iran and the Iranian people. It was stolen by the Shah! It is ours. It must not leave this country." He was appealing to the bank guard, who simply shrugged his hands and shoulders, gun pointing down at the floor now.

As they struggled, I took off. Bobby let go and went to the front door in one swift move, holding the door wide open for me. The two struggling for the box nearly fell over when Bobby released it. They were way off balance.

I sprinted past the maintenance cart like a full back waiting for a hand-off, arms wide open. I grabbed the toilet paper box firmly in a bear hug and dipped my head toward the door.

"Reeder! Follow and cover!" I yelled.

Although he was not in on the plan, he caught it quickly enough. Carter and Buell backed out behind him with guns covering the  lobby. Out the door I went toward the taxi.

There was a sport bike opposite me on the far curb. I could see the long, blond hair hanging from around the helmet. As the rider turned to look at me, I saw that it was Jennifer from my condo. She smiled and slowly pulled from under her coat an automatic pistol, aiming it right at my body. I froze in my tracks, knowing I was about to die in Iraq. She took careful, purposeful aim. I ducked my head, waiting for the inevitable slam and burn, then blackout.

Just then a shot rang out and Jennifer was knocked off her bike. The side of her pretty little head was gone. The shot came from inside the cab! The driver  was replacing his weapon in its holster when I and the three security jumped in though the open doors.

"Thanks, Man!" I said.

Colonel Reeder said, "I thought so, Mossad? I caught your accent coming over here."

The agent said, "Where to?"

"Karaj airport hanger six where you got us." He said,

"hanga six, roger that!"

We all laughed. Reeder slapped him on the shoulder.

"You must leave quickly now. Police will be all over soon."

"We've got a fast jet. Reeder punched his phone.

"Captain Wilson here."

"We are en route. ETA 8 minutes. Get runway clearance. Light the fires and kick the tires! Ask for clearance to directly to Flight Level 35 thousand, cause that's what we're going anyway! We've got to get out of Iraqi air space, pronto!"

"Got it, sir!" came the reply.

"You need to refuel? I can make arrangement in Tel Aviv for you, best in the region."

"Make it happen and thanks. You have been a great help, sir." Col. Reeder said after a brief thought, knowing he would have to use afterburners to clear Iranian air space if pursued.

## Chapter 7

Extraction. Jet fighter dogfight.
Intervention! An international
incident brewing.

As we pulled up to the plane, the jet engines were already whining. The staircase was lowered down and the copilot was there outside to help us aboard. He wondered about the box of toilet paper. "We've got plenty of that on board, sir."

"I doubt it!" and we all laughed.

"97617 N to the tower. Tower. Request clearance to FL35 from the runway."

There was a pause . "OK, checked all traffic. You are cleared to FL 35 97617 Nancy."

"97617, Roger that."

"You are Cleared to FL35 N97617".

"Roger that. N97617 out.

Door closed and locked.

"97617 Nancy, ready for takeoff." The pilot said to the tower.

"97617 Nancy, you are cleared to roll."

There was very little traffic. Throttles were pushed fully forward when the tower said alert,

alert, 97617 Nancy ABORT TAKE OFF, ABORT TAKE OFF! You are commanded to return to the gate at once! We say abort now.! 9671...

"Tower, you are breaking up," replied Captain Wilson as he rotated and applied the extra power this plane was equipped with to shoot directly up to 35,000 feet at 60 degrees, max climb rate.

"Man, I feel the G's, Colonel." I said to Reeder at my side.

"Yeah, after burners on this one."

"Really?" I exclaimed!"

***

"Scramble those fighters," came the order from the military man in charge. "I represent the council. Scramble and intercept 9617 Nancy. Force return to this air field at once."

"They are close to the border, sir. It seems that plane is very fast judging by our radar, sir."

"Scramble 'em now!" He barked!

Col Reeder went forward to the left hand pilot seat and said, "Captain Wilson, make for Vector airway to Tel Aviv. We will need fuel and have been cleared. Call ahead. We may soon have company up here. Make ready all diversion and avoidance systems."

"Roger that, sir; already done, sir., We will be out of Iranian air space in 7 minutes, sir."

"Good, but that's a lot of time for an F-16.

That's what they've got, thanks to us.!"

Nothing on screen yet, sir." He picked up the mic and called, "This is 97617 Nancy, Swiss Lear for Tel Aviv air control center, Do you read me?"

We already had 25,000 feet and climbing fast so we knew our signal would reach. The cab driver had just finished his top secret encrypted two way code 2 conversation with Tel Aviv tower.

"97617 Nancy , this is Tel Aviv tower?"

"Request landing coordinates and wind speed for unscheduled landing and refuel."

" 97617 Nancy, a squawk 2103 and proceed on Vector Airway 270 to Runway 25 Right. OK, we have you on radar now from your transponder squawk. Call again at 50 miles out 97617 N."

"Roger, 97617 out."

Almost at the same moment, "Colonel Reeder, sir, we have two bogies coming off the runway back at Karaj, climbing fast."

The whole scramble had been ordered so fast that the two F-16's were unarmed, only a cannon. No missiles were hung. But we did not know that "OK, launch chaff if needed."

"No missiles detected yet, sir."

"Roger that, Captain. Man, they are fast!"!

The F-16's were closing on our 6 . Just several nautical miles now, they fired a tracer round to parallel our nose and go past as a warning shot from their cannon. And pulled up alongside, each

side, showing the universal sign of a thumbs down ,
indicating to go back to the airfield. Holding up the
mic to indicate to switch back to the airfield channel on the radio. The pilot was waving it frantically.
Colonel Reeder and Captain Wilson could see that
there were no missiles mounted under their wings
but knew the F-16's could shoot us with their cannons and bring us down but that would probably
not retrieve the bonds for them. We were almost
out of the airspace now.

"Ok, seatbelts," Captain Wilson ordered to
Colonel Reeder, now!"

The colonel responded just in time. Captain
Wilson pulled up sharply and rolled the aircraft,
inverted around to the bottom and slightly rear of
the F-16's, releasing a volley of 50 caliber bullets
into their bellies. They were not prepared for this
from a private aircrafts. One lurched right and the
other left. Nothing vital like fuel tanks were hit.
Each rolled off and quickly maneuvered back onto
our 6. They were just about to light us up with their
cannons when two blurs and a thunderous roar
shook all of us.

Two Israeli F-18's strafed by, one on each side,
made a hard bank /360 and lit up the F-16 consoles
with the tell-tale missile lock! Knowing the Iranian
pilots would see and hear the lock tone. They knew
they were defenseless and peeled sharp left, and
took an immediate decent 500 feet out of pursuit

formation. They were bugging out as fighter jet jockeys say.

The Iranian military man in back at the airport tower was livid. Jumping up and down frustration with this outcome.

In a few seconds the Israeli Jets came back up to our side, paused and waved us forward, indicating they would escort us the rest of the way. We did not have their military radio frequency, but used the uniform hand code indicating we needed fuel.

"This is N 67167 Lear Jet calling Tel Aviv control."

"Tel Aviv control."

"We are 100 nautical miles out, Tel Aviv."

"N67167, we have you and your two friends, alongside. Come to runway 25 Right. You are cleared to land. Fuel is second turn off, right from the runway at 6500 foot roll."

"Roger that, Tel Aviv, runway 25 Right and 6500 foot roll, turn right for fuel."

The two jet escorts peeled off and accelerated past us now with a slight wing wave and disappeared up to the sound of their afterburners! We knew we were safe now!

We rolled 6500 feet and there was the second turn off. We taxied right and there was a fuel truck waiting. The first mate got out and directed the attendants to the fuel ports. The first mate handed over an International, Swiss bank Credit card for payment. In 46 minutes we were ready for take off.

"Tower, this is 96717N ready for takeoff. We are filing a flight plan direct for Geneva, Switzerland on Vector airways terminating at Zeitweiss General Aviation Airport. Request wind speed and procedure."

"This is the tower. Winds are 12 from 270 degrees. You are cleared for taxi to runway 10, N67167."

" Runway 10; Roger that."

When we got to the threshold of runway 10, the pilot called back to the tower. "N67167 requesting take off roll."

"This is the tower N16717. You are cleared. Go to FL 30. Have a good day!"

"Thank you, tower. Thanks for all your help. We are rolling."

" Roger that, N16717."

The jet accelerator levers were pushed forward and we were on our way to Switzerland. *Another one of those radical takeoffs! Whew! What a morning!.*

"Colonel Reeder, please contact Dr. Bern and tell him we are en route and confer with the pilot for an ETA. We will need to be picked up at the field. Also will you ask the co-pilot to come back and talk to me when he has a chance?"

"Roger that sir," came the reply.

The co-pilot came to the back of the plane and sat beside me. "Yes sir, how can I help you?"

"Do you guys still carry a flight case with your charts and Navigation gear?"

"Oh yes, sir, every pilot has one. It's like an appendage."

"About like this?" I used my hands to illustrate. He nodded his head affirmatively. "Ok, good. I will need to create a little diversion when we get to our destination...."

"Sir.... ?"

"Well, here's the thing. We've had agents of various kinds and nationalities following us all the way here from back, days ago in Washington DC. There was a girl on a motorcycle back there at the bank that was shot just before she could shoot me. That girl was in my apartment building hallway, just days ago. I have come to learn how ubiquitous surveillance has become in our world."

He was shaking his head in agreement.

"Now, we have bearer bonds on board this plane . They won't be safe until they are actually in the hands of Dr. Bern and the banking system. That's why we have such a security team as an escort and they are well armed indeed. They are our vanguard."

"Yes, Yes, sir , I understand. We work together

all the time."

"Ok good, But, I am going to need you to help me with a deception as we disembark this airplane. I am sure those Iranian folks who were chasing us in those military jets—incidentally, you two pilots did a remarkable maneuver to evade and attack back there!"

"Thanks, we're both ex-military pilots."

"Anyway, they will have will have alerted all agents here. No doubt there are some."

His eyes were enlarging.

"These bonds are like a golden football, and the whole other team will run interference and any maneuver to get their hands on it. Understand?" I looked deep into his eyes without a blink, to convey the intensity and the gravity of what was at stake here.

"Yes sir, I think I understand. But what can I do, Sir?"

"Well, we we're going to use a fake handoff and an end around run, Bill—you are Bill, right?"

"Yes, sir, Bill Simpson."

"Oh, great!" I said. "Don't jump over any chairs inside. I want you to just walk calmly as you guys usually do. Kind of apart from the passengers. You know, like your job as a pilot is done for the day. But you will have the ball in your flight bag!"

Like a director now, I said, "You are just ambling in with your flight bag and its charts, books, binders and the like, going in a different direction, apart from your passengers. We will be in a phalanx, surrounded by security looking all purposeful and determined, a quick step like we have the ball and must protect it."

He was shaking his head affirmatively.

"I take it you have transportation here?"

"Yes sir, I ride a Vespa scooter."

" Wow!" I said as I got a mental picture of him, in uniform; hat on and his flight bag in the middle of the floor of the Vespa between his legs. *Perfect!*

"I went to your on board copier and copied the first serial number and the last of that series of bonds. If anybody were to get them I can have them decayed and worthless. Of course, I am sorry to say that you will be dead."

He didn't see the humor. "OK, so far. Then what do I do?"

"You leave the airport, don't speed, cross the village direct to Dr. Bern's bank. Go to the entrance at the back down that small alleyway. Know where I mean?"

"Ya, Ya." he said.

"We will have taken a more circuitous route through the north side of the village to determine if we have a tail If we draw any fire, you will already have delivered the goods to Dr. Bern. I will alert him to meet you at the back door. It will be getting to dusk by then. "What do ya think, Bill, can you pull this off ?"

"Ya, Ya, dis is de piece of cake, no problem for me."

"Extra pay, Bill," I affirmed, nodding. "Hazard pay!"

"Dis is gut. I know every alleyway on my Vespa. Where auto can't go!"

"Great. Bring me your flight bag back here. Like you are showing me a chart of the landing pattern. I will place the size of 2 bricks inside. Not heavy. Hold that chart out in your hand for all to see as you work your way back to me. I'll be ready." I had moved the bonds from the toilet box to my briefcase when we took on fuel.

He came bounding back, excited to show me his chart. I slipped the bonds into his flight case. "Let's hope this works as well as it did at the bank," I said under my breath.

We made great ceremony over the chart. I was a pilot in my early days VFR. But I did not know what I was looking at. I must remember to call Dr. Bern and bring him up to date, that his security co-pilot would be bringing the bonds to his back door on a Vespa and not with the full security contingent. Timing would be critical.

We set down and taxied to the General Aviation staging area. We had just stopped and shut down the engines when a dark grey sedan and a military vehicle pulled up to greet us.

We dropped the stairs and began to deplane. The military man, a Lieutenant Colonel, I believe, came forward and introduced himself. His two comrades were walking around the plane looking, it seemed, for damage. They noticed that the Lear 75 had been modified with a cannon and anti missile hardware. Also, afterburners.

"Wow!" They said. "We've never seen one like this before."

"It belongs to me... or my Bank," came another voice from the Grey sedan. Dr. Bern and another man were now walking up to the plane. The other man was some kind of national police, like our FBI.

"Hello, Dr. Bern !, I said, it is so good to see you again."

"Hello, Mr. Charles. It is good to see that you made it safely back to friendly soil."

"Ah, there could be a bullet hole or two, sir as we evaded those fighters."

"Yes Michael, I heard all radio transmissions. Good pilots, Michael."

"They sure are," I said.

Dr. Bern turned to the lieutenant colonel, and re-introduced himself, asking if he could be of assistance.

"Well, Sir, we picked up radio transmissions and had radar tracking on this plane. There was a pursuit by two fighter jets as it approached and departed Iranian air space."

Dr. Bern was nodding, "Ya, Ya."

And then the lt. col. said, "That's not all, sir. We then observed two other military jets, we think Israeli in origin, we don't know because we cannot receive radio transmissions from our military, come to the assistance of your plane in maneuvers which caused the Iranian jets to turn and run! They were , by then, out of their airspace," he added.

"Ya, Ya," said Dr. Bern shaking his head, as though he were waiting for a punch line. "Is there a complaint, Colonel?", he said as though this were routine with him.

"Well, no Sir. Not actually. We would like to know what is at issue here that this pursuit was necessary. We are going to have to answer to officials."

"Ah, Yes, Colonel, I thoroughly understand." He reached in his pocket and drew out a card, handing it to the military man, he said, "By all means, please have them call me at my office. There is no contraband on board."

The other man with Dr. Bern stepped a few steps forward, parting his coat, slightly, revealing a badge of some kind, I did not recognize, but the colonel must have  as his response was a quick, "Yes, Sir." If there was, he didn't want to know about it.

I motioned for the co-pilot to come over to where we were standing. He acknowledged me and began to move in our direction. Quickly, I said,"Dr. Bern, may I have a word with you?"

"Of course, Michael," moving a few feet away from the others.

"I would like you to meet," just as the copilot came to us. "This is Bill, our copilot."

"Yes, of course I know Bill."

"Oh, good. I am hoping you won't mind if Bill and two of your security men rode back to the bank with you and then can you send a car back here with him for his scooter out here in the parking lot?"

"Vell, yes, I suppose so," with some hesitation.

Bill exclaimed, "Oh good, I'll just get my chart bag from the plane."

I winked at Dr. Bern with my back to all others. "You will have everything you need, Dr."

He seemed to have a tentative understanding. He knew I was up to something. Maybe a little sub-terfuge. He was going to trust it.

Bill came out with his chart bag looking very normal and made for the grey sedan. Dr. Bern nudged his police official to indicate to follow Bill and secure him. The agent understood, and fell in behind him. All looked innocuous.

Both secure now in the back, Col. Reeder strolled over and looked at me with curiosity.

"Oh Colonel," I said, "can you deploy 2 of your men to ride with Dr. Bern back to his bank?"

He nodded his head in silence and walked back to where they were waiting at the ready, witnessing all of these developments. A few words and they walked slowly over to the grey sedan. Right then, a sort of a Hum Vee vehicle pulled up. It was Col. Reeder's driver and usual transportation. He yelled out, "Ok, men, let's get this cargo to its owner, cross town," in a loud voice.

I bolted for the plane and retrieved my brief-case. I took a pair of hand cuffs, I knew were in the plane, and cuffed the briefcase to my wrist.

Back outside, I waved to Dr. Bern and made my way straight for the Hum Vee. Security followed and secured me inside. I was glad that Dr. Bern, hearing the Lear's radio had come out to meet us. This eliminated a lot of exposure on Bill's Vespa. Now he had the bonds.

Dr. Bern turned to Bill the co-pilot in his car and said, "Do you have something for me, son?"

Bill was nervous and said, "Are you the Dr. Bern I was supposed to meet at the back door of you bank on my scooter?"

Dr. Bern laughed out loud and said, "I hadn't got that message yet, but yes, that's me. Do you have the bonds?"

"I think so sir they are in my flight bag here. "

He partially opened it for Dr. Bern to see. He looked in and recognized the size of the black paper wrapped package . "Ah gut, just leave them in there until we are safe inside my bank. Michael may know something we don't. He leaned forward and said, "Full Alert, men"

We took a completely different route out of the airport and headed across town. I sat with the briefcase handcuffed to my wrist between my legs. Very visible.

I heard an overhead sound . It was very loud and getting louder by the second. Then I felt the wind buffeting the HumVee. Col. Reeder yelled out "Chopper, Chopper! 12 o'clock!"

The chopper and it's full weight pressed down on the top of the Hum Vee as a deployment team landed all around us. Out came the automatic weapons, shots were fired until we realized that we were completely surrounded and outnumbered. Col. Reeder indicated no joy by raising his gun in open hand. He turned to me and yelled. "Did you do what I think you did?"

"Yes sir," was my quick response.

"Ok , let me handle this!"

The back doors were opening, I had my cuff key in hand. Guns were pointed at my head. I waved my free hand in surrender and held up my key to the cuffs. The gun was jerked to indicate 'move the key and unlock the cuffs or I would die'. I did so quickly. The briefcase was grabbed. I heard a siren in the background. It was some distance away, but enough for the assault team to exercise precision as the chopper moved 10 feet forward and almost to the ground, while the team re-entered the chopper and it ascended sharply, avoiding all power lines.

I didn't want to be accessible when they discovered my case's contents. Col. Reeder had the same thought and ordered the driver, "Safe Compound, now!"

The driver made a hard left turn, saying, "Sir!" We sped, we made several hard turns, then under a building, as if a parking garage were underneath. Down a ramp and level, when a the light behind us got dark, as a giant door slid into place and locked. The driver came to a halt. Doors popped open and we all got out.

"OK, Charles, Does Dr. Bern have the bonds"? Yes sir, I said.

"Are you sure?" " They left with him, Sir. " Reeder got on his radio, he had to be careful what he said over the air. He called the two agents that accompanied Dr. Bern and using pre-determined code asked about their status. The message he got in return meant all was secure at their destination, now. His relief was visible.

# Chapter 8

## Swiss Bank and Swiss Chalet

"Good call, Mr. Charles. Follow me, you two," meaning me and Bobby. He hadn't quite recovered from the assault. And so we did, through two security doors and came into a spacious and fairly luxurious office. "Wanna' a drink?" He moved to a bar on the left. There was an attendant, a bartender. "Jack and water," I said.

Bobby asked, "Do you have Tequila?"

He hit me on the shoulder and said "All this for nothing! Now I don't have any Bonds, We have come half way around the world..."

I stopped him, holding my hand up. The ruse had escaped him, "Bobby, Dr. Bern has the bonds now!" I said.

He hunched his shoulders and became wide-eyed. "What? What? They got the briefcase!"

" Yes, that's true. I thought somebody might try, so I put them in the co-pilot's chart case and he went with Dr. Bern."

"No? Man, really?" He smiled his big white smile kind of laughing in disbelief.

"Yeah, really!"

"I wondered why you gave it up so easily! Even though there were guns..."

"There was nothing in that briefcase. "

As the truth began to sink in... "Wow, ah man," he exclaimed. Repeatedly.

I said, "Stay sharp, we are not out of it yet."

"Ok, man."


Col. Reeder walked up, ordered a scotch and said, "Good move, Mr. Charles."

"Oh, you knew"? interjected Bobby.

"We were in a bad place with that assault team. Who were they"?

"Don't know yet, sir" Just a percentage call. But they're goanna be pissed now, When they open that case. I'd like to have two of your guys with us for the next several days."

"You got it," he said. "I like the way you move, Charles. If you ever need a job..."

"Thanks, Sir, but when our transaction is completed, I hope to be able to retire. That will depend on the expertise of Dr. Bern now; but I am honored.


We sped around town and through some alleyways, checking for a tail. Finally, we came to a large warehouse, old and somewhat dingy outside. The door started sliding right to give us entry. I realized our driver was controlling its movement. Dark for about 30 feet, we went through a second partition. On the other side it was well lit, clean and modern. We continued in an S pattern and then 2-3 hundred feet . We pulled into another square room and the door closed behind us. It was a heavy door and you could hear it lock in a firm manner. "Well, men," Col. Reeder said as he opened his door, "Well done."

I sensed some finality to their mission for now. Everyone got out and we followed the group as we went through a glass double door and behold, there was an elevator. We all went inside. We went up two floors and the colonel opened the door to a large lobby with a number of people going about their business. Then he closed the door and pressed the 10th floor. "You see, gentleman, this is the bank."

We were both surprised by this quiet and beautiful business setting as contrasted with the wild street experience we had just encountered. You could see the relief in our faces and eyes. The colonel chuckled.

The elevator's next stop was just as exciting. A spacious office, modern furniture, a large conference table. We noticed a display of shrimp and other assorted goodies on a beautifully decorated table next to a bar with a bar tender. Some Dom

Perignon was chilling. From around the corner came a loud clap! "Velcome gentlemen! Hello, Michael," he came over to give me a hug. "And this must be Mr. King, nephew of the Shah.". Bobby extended his hand and they shook hardily. "You look like your uncle. You know, I knew him long ago."

"No, I didn't know."

"Of course, you wouldn't, you would have been very young. Your uncle used to bank here, among other places, of course."

"I see," said Bobby.

"In fact, we may have sold him some of your bonds originally. They have our bank mark on them. We are still checking all of them but so far it looks really gut."

Well, I just stood there, smiling like a Jackass at all this but was glad for the coincidence . Dr. Bern had never mentioned this to me.

"I can assure you, your bonds will be safe here in our safe. Ve even have some of the Crown Jewels of several Royal Families in Europe here.

"Now, make yourselves at home. Have something to eat. There is champagne if you like and Stevern behind the bar will get you whatever you would like. You have been through a great deal in the past 24 hours. Ve watch all on monitor.!

"There has been some attention from the news media. BBC. They are just waking up to the reports of the little jet dogfight you all put on. Lots of questions coming.

Just then, my phone rang.

"Hello?"

"Damnit it, Dad, was that you two I am hearing about on the morning news here? Something about a dog fight, in jets, escaping Iranian air space and two F18 fighter jets from Israel coming to your aid. Shots fired. After burners and all that crap! You ought to hear it. They know who you are, you know!"

"Oh really?" I said.

"Oh yeah, they got you two boarding the plane out of Dulles and then they are showing examples of the Lear 75. There are computer animations of the dog fight and firing sequences." Her voice grew louder.

"Now honey, I am perfectly safe here in Switzerland, at the bank.:

"See? I knew that was you and your buddy. There is a lot of conjecture in the Media about every aspect of what you all are doing! And why. Well, I am glad to hear your safe now. I am sure it won't be long until they find me as your daughter."

"Just tell `em that they have the wrong guy and that I am an old man who has trouble walking."

"Yeah, sure!"

"Honey, I have to go now. I'll call back tonight and let you know when I am coming home."

"You better come from under a rock or you are

going to have a lot of press ready to greet you two. I am glad you're all right. But you're still half a world away. Be careful"

I had drawn aside and now returned to the group. The co-pilot had joined all of us and was sharing in the celebration. He joked about how it was going to be telling his grandchildren about how he once had over a billion dollars in his chart case.
"

Ok, Mr. Charles, Mr. King, Ve have some business to discuss. Please,if you will, be seated at the table here for a few moments," said Dr. Bern as we moved to an out of the way table in a nook of his office. We both responded, and sat down. To pad, pen and ice water.

Dr. Bern began, "Gentleman, I have had a chance to review randomly about 25 of your bonds and check their serial numbers. Did you know some of them were Peruvian Bonds?"

"No," Bobby returned.

"They are of special value and very rare. They all check out, so far. I am waiting for all of the bonds to be counted and audited. There is a great deal of money here, considering two things 1.) The increase in the value of spot gold to today's price and; 2.) The 'Art' value as artifacts or art objects; probably in the billions of dollars and I have already contacted some very wealthy people who have expressed an interest in some of them. You may wish to liquidate a small part of them to obtain some useable cash now and invest long term with the rest."

We both shook our heads, silently, in agreement.

"And there is the matter of our security detail and expenses related to your, ah, extraction, shall we call it?"

"Oh, yes," we said in unison.

"We will leave the negotiation with private parties to you, Dr. Bern, to pay all bills related to our security until we are safely home in the US, or other; air plane fee's, fuel ,etc, please deduct the customary commission for yourself for this negotiation of sale. We would like to net $100 million each"—I looked over at Bobby for his consent—"for ourselves to be held at your bank here in accounts, nominated to each of us separately. We would like to have a Visa and American Express cards attached to each account for spending. These accounts will also be used for any and all future distributions of funds from any future investments proceeds. It is an emulation account, and can not be related in any way to the master account, in which your bonds are secured. Now, let's see, do you have a branch bank in New York?" I asked.

"Yes, Yes," he said. "Also, there is a Federal Roll Program just now organizing by the Fed, with some major corporations participating, in a 500 M Escrow. Returns are expected to be roughly 20% per month, as the series notes are sold.

"Can we get into that in time Dr. Bern?" I said.

"I think so, Michael. Ve vill try. I have already reserved a position for you."

"Wow!, that would be a nice return!"

"Of course, you must sign these non-disclosure agreements," he slid them across the table for us to execute.

"Routine." I said glancing at Bobby. He nodded and signed.

"Dr. Bern, I think that concludes everything for now. Except for one thing."

"Yes Michael?"

"What would be appropriate, how would I thank... that is, acknowledge the participation and essential aid of the Israeli air force and the Mossad on the ground. One saved my life."

Dr. Bern held up his hand, stopping me. "Leave that up to me, Michael. I will see to it."

"Oh, good." I said

Bobby head, up and down enthusiastically. "And a gratuity for our security team sir."

"Yes, Yes, OK. The Victor can afford to be generous! Eh!"

"Now, what else? Dr. Bern must have made a call because a young man appeared with two slender leather portfolios. He opened them up and presented them to each of us with our credit card accounts. These cards were guilt edged with Gold, their folders made by GUCCI leather design.

"Gee, it's nice to go first class, hey, Bob?" I said.

"Yes, this is so nice, Michael. How do you know these people?"

"Long story, tell you on the way home.

"Now, where will you go from here, gentleman? You are both welcome to stay at my Chalet in the mountains for as long as you like. Great skiing! I can fly you up there. Stevern will see to all your needs. This might not be the time to return home with the current media interest. Maybe a week to allow for other news to intervene. Right now, It looks like you would be mobbed by the press. Really, just too dangerous. There are other interests, internationally, that want to lay claim to these assets. This will give our attorneys an opportunity to get in front of this legally, before any statements are made."

"Whatever you think is best, Dr. Bern.".

Bobby nodded agreement. Bobby added, "I would love to ski there, Dr. Bern and we are ready to leave at any time."

"OK , Good, I will arrange it. Col. Reeder will escort you, after lunch.

"Hey Bobby, don't you feel a little lighter now

that we have those bonds safely put away and have our account cards for all we could spend for the rest of our lives!" I bumped him in the shoulder!

"Man, in my wildest dreams, I couldn't imagine such a thing."

"Get some security. And a driver. It will be well known what you have now! You will need an indoctrination of what you must be aware of now, for yourself and your family. There will be attempts to exploit, even kidnap, Col. Reeder will explain it to you on our trip up."

The colonel was within earshot and I looked over at him for confirmation.

"Sure,: he said. "These precautions should be in place as soon as possible, with the crazy media."

"Kali?"

"Yeah, Dad How are you?"

"Oh good! Fabulous actually! I am worth at least 100 million dollars. which will accrue to you and Sean. We are rich, girl! Now this is important. I need to go to Dr. Bern's ski chalet like last time. We want interest to cool down a little before I return.

"Here is what I want you to do. I am wiring to your account at Regions, the one I used to use to give you a few bucks..."

"Yeah?"

"Ok, I am sending $10 grand . I want you all to leave for Disney World as soon as possible. Just get

Sean, his family and walk out the door. The money will be there and useable on your debit card in 30 minutes. Don't talk to anyone. Don't tell the kids. We now must take many security precautions, kidnapping, etc. check in with cash and give a false name. In fact, use my old corporate name Vacom, Inc."

"Ok , dad, this is getting a little weird. We do have jobs, you know?"

"Family emergency! You really don't have to work anymore."

"You mean I can kick these shoes off?The ones I walk miles of hospital hallways every day?"

"Your choice, go to medical school if you want." Just keep a low profile for now."

"Ok, I got it."

"Yeah, just drive over and check in. The Colonial is great. Call me back tonight when you get settled. Ok, be alert!"

"Ok , bye."

*Ooooo Hahhh, yow wee!* Arms, flying.

"What going on, Mom?" The kids said.

"Whew! Everybody down here in the living room." Exited calls upstairs were made. Two minutes later, all were assembled. "Ok. Kids, and Carlos—Dad—we are going to Disney."

"Oh good," they jumped up and down, "When?" they shouted.

"How about right now? Just grab one outfit, your bathing suit and we will buy everything else when we get there. Meet me back down here in 10 minutes."

Carlos came over and said, "What's going on?"

"Dad is sending 10 grand for us to go hide at Disney. We must be a little incognito. I'll explain in the car. We could be in danger if we stay here right now."

"Ok, I am in," said Carlos, "I've got vacation time accrued."

"Oh, I forgot, you won't have to work anymore . Maybe you could open that Fish & Bait shop you always wanted to. Dad's worth 100 million now. We are all millionaires!"

Carlos stood for a second. frozen while that sunk in.

"We have to go now," said Kali.

The kids came downstairs very excited. "Ok, check list," the oldest daughter said.

"No, no checklist needed," Kali said. "Just grab your suit, one pair of shorts and a top. Flip flops and we are outt`a here! Tell you in the car!"

Everyone jumped in the big Pacifica. "I need a snack," the young ones were protesting.

"Ok, we will get you all something. Just be patient. Carlos, honey, stop by Regions, I need to get us some cash. As they were passing through the Iron privacy gates of the development, they could see in the distance a Channel 10 news truck approaching. Kali had a hunch, but the other's didn't think anything of it,

They pulled up to the drive thru ATM and Kali punched in for a balance. It came back 10,320.00 She withdrew 1,000 , that was the daily limit. She didn't want to go inside, so that would do for the 2 hour drive. "Ok, let's go."

She called ahead to the Colonial Hotel.""Yes, I would like two adjoining rooms for 1 week, for tonight, in fact we are heading there now. About two hours. Ok , please call me back, you have my number on caller ID."

"Ok, stop at this Circle K on the corner. Now kids, lets go in and get some goodies. Candy, chips, whatever you want for the trip. Now don't fill up because we will stop at Mickey Dee's on the way over."

Mickey Dee's was the shout from all!

*Wow! Just in the  nick of time,* Kali thought. *Once this gets out these kids will not be safe. This changes everything!* She would ask her dad about it tonight.

"Jack?"

"Hey, dad."

"Whatsup? I saw the news."

"Yeah, well that's why I am calling. You are a multi-millionaire now. Got some sick time at work?"

"Yeah!"

"The news media will be there in no time. Your family could be in danger after that. I am arranging for security from here. But listen, here's what I want you to do immediately! You and Cewena and Carson grab a bathing suit, underwear change and 1 outfit—shorts, I imagine. Go straight to your credit union. I have sent 10 grand for you to go directly to Disney. Already called Kali. Go to the Colonial where you will meet her. Leave now. I will call you tonight. Now! 5 minutes."

"Got it, Dad."


As they pulled through the iron security gate, there was a news van at the automatic registry scanning the names. The young female reporter was heard to say "Oh, they both live here! In this development."

Sean silently went through on the other side and exited onto the access road.


Now Cewena hadn't been told much. She said, "Sean, now tell me what this is all about."

"Well, did you see that news truck? They were

coming for us. They would have painted a target and bull's-eye on our family. Dad pulled off a deal in Iran worth billions! We are now millionaires and could be in danger from many sides for a while Kids have been kidnapped for ransom . He needs time to get security in place and so he is sending us to Disney World for a week or so. He sent us 10 grand. It's at the Credit Union, so first stop ATM. If they are still open, well go inside. ATM has a limit."

"Is that what I caught on the news earlier.?"

"Yeah. Let's go." They passed another news truck on the way another half a mile down the road, heading for their development. Their entry gate was the only thing down that road.

Dr. Bern walked back in from his inner office and said, "Michael, Mr. King, you must excuse me there are many pressing matters I must attend to."

We nodded agreement.

"Col. Reeder will accompany you to my Chalet. Helmut is the Butler/caretaker and he will meet you and see to your needs. I am sending a car to the local airstrip to bring you in. Have a wonderful time and call me if you need anything. Oh, and the phone lines are secure. I vill be in touch with additional developments on the bonds. Now I must go".

There were the traditional embraces and thank you's and Dr. Bern disappeared into his inner office.

Col. Reeder said, "We have had a surveillance team check a three block radius and our friends seem to have left the immediate area. I am certain they know we no longer have the bearer bonds in our possession, so I do not think there will be trouble, although I am sure they will be angry, finding nothing in your briefcase. We can leave for the Chalet whenever you are ready". It's just a short chopper ride away.

After lunch we went to the private elevator in the office which led us straight up to a platform even with the roof of our building. On there was our ride.

It was a Bell 407 GX, Executive configuration with plenty of room for six passengers. Dr. Bern sure did know how to ride. Col. Reeder ushered us over to the side door and in we went. It was beautifully appointed in fine soft leather inside. "Gentleman, please be seated in the rear, for balance. I will sit up with the pilot for even weight distribution. This flight will be approximately 45 minutes.

I turned to Bobby and said, "Do you need to call home? We should stay here a week or so, to allow the press and the story to settle down or we will be mobbed when we get back to Washington."

"Yes, I will call my daughter."

"I have already sent my children and their families into hiding. Sort of, that is. I sent them to Disney World under factious names. I think the press was closing in. Is she still in the hospital?"

"No, home now.".

"Can she travel?" I asked.

"Yes, I think so."

"Tell Ya what I did. I wired money to their bank account and told them to get outt'a dodge, immediately. Take practically nothing. By what you need there. Use a fake name, pay cash. Enjoy and I'll call later."

"But why,?" Bobby said.

"From what my daughter told me, the press picked up on our little dog fight with the Iranians and the Israeli jets who just happened to be there to drive them off. Why were they patrolling so close, etc. They have video of us boarding at Dulles. You know the press, when in doubt, exploit! It won't take them long to find our relatives, to interview. This could expose them to unsavory types, who when they find out about these newly found riches , may kidnap for ransom. We need to talk to Col. Reeder about an on-going security scheme for both of us. Being rich has its own responsibilities."

"Oh yeah," Bobby nodded affirmatively. "I see. Oh yeah. I will call now."

"Don't send her to another relative's house. Give her a vacation! But she must pay cash and use an alias. How about a cruise? Alaska, that'll take a while."

"Yes, good. I am calling now."

Col. Reeder interjected, "I was planning to have this discussion with you all at the Chalet, but I have associates back in the US and can send coverage at any time. They will stay in the background until such time as we work out a permanent strategy."

"That sounds great to me, sir."

"Where are your people?"

"A son and daughter, four children staying at the Colonial Hotel in Disney. I can give you room numbers tonight."

"I' am on it now!"

"Thanks, very much."

Bobby chimed in, "My sister is at 127 North Washington Ave, in Bethesda, MD."

"Ok, got it," he said . "You guys will be covered in an hour. It will cost about 10 grand per month, travel included. And extra personnel, when needed."

"I' am in for that," I said.

"Does that include me and my sister?"

"Yeah, we can work that out."

We both breathed a sigh of relief. It was getting a little dark and I could see the Chalet, well lit and sitting atop a clearing, nearly on the mountaintop. I could see the Hilo Pad just behind the main house. It had not been there when I last stayed there several years ago.

There was a call to Dr. Bern. "Sir, we believe you may have been entrusted with certain Germen Barer Bonds from my country, Iran," he began, "by a nephew of the former Shah."

There was silence on Dr. Bern's side of the phone. "Who am I speaking to, please?"

"This is Ankar Ali Belzer, I am the ambassador for the Inner Council of the Loyal Sons of Iran. These bonds belong to our country. They were stolen and we demand their return, immediately!"

"Mr. Belzer, I am not certain I am familiar with these Bonds you mention. When did this occur? Our bank is not in the habit of accepting stolen assets!"

"Sir, it was last night! We chased and then tracked a jet, Lear 75 , back to the airport in Geneva. It is registered to your bank, Sir."

"My secretary, Mrs. Hollinger, will take your contact information. I will refer you to our attorney for international affairs, when I have been able to verify this allegation. Would you be kind enough to fax me your letterhead to 013 446-0778 as soon as possible, please, Mr. Belzer. I assure you, I vill look into this, immediately!" *Humph*! He said under his breath when he had hung up. *Attorney Whilomwill tie these character's up for many years.*

As we drew closer to the Chalet, I could make

out Stevern frantically waving us in. He was there when I last stayed. It would be good to see him again. A very high energy individual, he was exceptional at what he did there. Both an accomplished chef and world-class skier, he was well known in the small ski town. There was nothing he couldn't get for you. This was going to be a fun stay.

We centered on the crosshairs of the pad and descended to a soft touch. Stevern opened the Ranger's door.

"Hello, Michael!" he exclaimed with much enthusiasm. "It is very gut to see you again . Welcome, Welcome! And who is this?"

"This is Bobby."

"Welcome, Bobby, I am Stevern and I will see to your every need. Come now Gentlemen, are you hungry?"

"Oh yeah!" we said in unison.

"Gut, I have a Chateau Briand prepared. It will be ready in a few minutes. Freshen up and I will have some chilled red wine for you. Jon, inside, will show you to your quarters. I will see you right after you are settled.There is a play in the village tonight if you feel up to it."

"Stevern, you're still number one," I said and shook his hand again.

Jon came in the room, was introduced and he showed us upstairs to our quarters. "Just tell me if you need anything, sirs."

"Ok," we replied"

A call was put through to my room. I picked up the phone and was surprised to hear Dr, Bern on the other end. "Hello, Michael, are you settled in?"

"Oh yes Heinz. All is excellent , as usual."

"Ah, gut. I am calling because there have been some developments related to your assets and their removal from Iran."

Yes?" I said, listening for more.

"They are claiming through their ambassador here that you and the Shah's nephew, Bobby, stole these assets from their country. And that they are a national treasure and stolen, originally, from the Iranian people by the Shah himself. And, of course , the whole world has seen the news footage and computer simulation of the jet dog fight you were engaged in and the Israeli intervention on your behalf. There are many sensitive elements to your venture. I am hearing from many different national agencies, including your deputy Secretary of State. Of, course I have told them nothing. I just want to warn you that you and Mr. King are in for some very serious interrogation when you get back home."

"Yes sir. Thank you so much for the heads up Dr. Bern. I have reviewed our security options with Col Reeder and have made some preliminary arrangements, already. Do you know of a good International Attorney with a shingle in Geneva and the U. S?"

"Yes and I am faxing you names and contacts already. He does work for our bank and is very knowledgeable. He will protect both of you. Do what he tells you. I will brief him tomorrow on this whole affair. The bank will engage and pay him for his services. You may have some participation."

"OK," I said.

"I don't think their allegations are actionable in our courts, but you must watch out for your own safety. These people are unscrupulous, Michael."

"Yes, Sir, and thank you for your kind hospi-tality."

"Now, you are sure you have told me every-thing, Michael?"

"Yes, Sir, to the letter. The box was in Bobby's Iranian name. It was verified before my very eyes by the teller. There was an attempt to steal it right out of our hands in the bank lobby. If it weren't for a little deception, they would have gotten it."

"Ok, Michael, do not worry. Let's hope this does not turn into an international incident."

"With the current climate of affairs between these countries, the purpose for the credit blocking was nefarious. I could not be involved in it. Nor Bobby," I added.

"Let's eat!"

When we came downstairs, Stevern had prepared in a superb setting for our Briand and Roth-schild Burgundy. The dining room was adorned with a unique gold chandelier, and deep red cherry furniture. What a treat! And we were hungry after our long journey. More so than we knew.

"Of course we don't keep TV in the dining room, but you two are quite the celebrities, I see," said Stevern. "You are on every news show. Quite a stir! I love the way our plane out maneuvered those Iranian jets."

"Yes, but were it not for the Israelis running them off in their F18's, we would have been toast on the next maneuver"

"I think we were out of their air space," said Bobby.

"Yeah, like that would matter. But they would not have been able to retrieve the bearer bonds from a burning aircraft." Stevern added.

"I was talking to Dr. Bern on the phone up-stairs. He has heard from their Ambassador, who is claiming a theft of national assets. Dr. Bern has hired an international law firm already."

"Those bonds were left to me," interjected Bob-by.

"It is just a claim, a lie. You have your paper-work," I said. "They are seeing red that it was the Israelis that came to our aid. You know how rela-tions are between those two!"

Stevern was listening intently.

"The talking heads are having a field day with conjecture on the news stations. BBC leading off," Stevern said.

"Hear that, Bobby? We're famous"!

"Ah don't know 'Ke-mo sah-bee'!"

We all laughed., and turned our glasses up.

"Seriously though," came a warning tone from Col. Reeder, standing in the corner. "Better watch your asses!" He brought us back to reality. "There are some nasty people you've awakened. These folks believe you have what is theirs. Your families will not be safe for some time to come."

This was beginning to sound scary. It was putting a pall on our celebration. I saw Bobby's smile disappear, replaced by a furrow of his brow as he became introspective.

We decided to get outside into the village. A pub was located at the bottom of the mountain. We had a Grog and then I said, "Let's go skiing!"

I knew the exercise would improve our prospective.

"Beginners' slopes first," Bobby said. "These are big mountains!"

"Yeah, I agree," I said. "Let's clear it with Col. Reeder this time."

Back up the hill now, we headed out the door. Colonel Reeder we found right outside of the Grog Shack, standing watch.

"Oh, we didn't know you were here outside," I said.

"Naturally," replied the colonel.

"Whattya think about us going skiing on the beginners slopes?"

"Well, things are still heating up from the reports I am getting. I wouldn't be able to protect you out there on the slopes from a party who wishes you harm."

"How would they know we are here?"

"Dr. Bern is a very public figure. They will cover all the bases. Eventually, agents will show up here. I will be forewarned. We have a great theater built into the Chalet. How about a movie?"

"Yes, Sir," we both sung out. "A movie, Sir!"

He got into the car with us and the driver made haste to return to the Chalet.

"We chose an old favorite, 'Top Gun', from the library. A 1988 film with great sound effects. Dr. Bern's home theater was superbly appointed and equipped. A truly unique sound system. I began to wonder who and what people may have been guests in these very seats.

When we came back upstairs, Stevern had a night cap ready for us. A Tia Maria on the rocks. I knew this was going to aid in my sleep. Bobby and I drank heartily, thanked him and went upstairs.

I opened the chalet's double French doors out

onto a balcony from my third-story room. What a view! The ski slopes were cast in white light where snow machines and grooming equipment were working. The main lodge was brightly illuminated, nestled at the bottom of the double chair lifts that were visible. People were still on the slopes as they were lighted near the lodge.

There was a little village of condo's, deep set in the valley, with cobblestone streets and gas lights, reminiscent of a by-gone era. The air was crisp and icy.

*What a winter scene. Idyllic, every child's Christmas village image. Probably designed that way,* I reflected.

I found myself wondering what my children and grandchildren were doing tonight at Disney, half a world away, hoping for something NEW in the news cycle. Better call them. What time was it back there? Oh, kind'a late there now. *First thing in the morning,* I told myself. I was becoming home-sick for them.

# Chapter 9

## Deputy Secretary of State
## and a free ride home

My old phone was ringing deep within my briefcase. I'd grown accustomed to using the secure phone Col. Reeder had given me to use. The call must be from someone who had the old number. Maybe family. I'd never get to it in time before it went automatically to voice box. It only allowed about three to four rings. But the number would be archived and perhaps there would be a message left to listen to. And then, there was the time zone difference. I vowed that I'd look at it and the incoming calls later.

It rang again. *Ok, better get it out and see who was so persistent at this hour back in the US.* Click, click, the brief case. Purge the call history. No , not the kids, good. THE US STATE DEPARTMENT . Oh Crap! Call back number, automatic press.

"Deputy Secretary of State, Omar Jackson. Hello, Mr. Charles. I assume that's you from my caller I.D."

"Yes Sir, this is Mr. Charles. How can I help

you, sir?"

"Well, sir, the recent events over the past two days have given us some cause for alarm here at the State Department. We are vitally interested in what has transpired in your negotiations with Iranian officials."

"Well sir, I am not sure you would call them officials, but..."

"Sir," he broke in, "when they scramble two F-16's to intercept your aircraft , believe me , they were Officials!"

"Yes sir, you've got a point there. I guess you could say they were chasing us."

"Mr. Charles, it looked from here that if it weren't for the aid and intervention of the Israeli Air Force, you would have in all probability been shot down."

"Sir, we did have some defenses on..." I stopped short, realizing that I was going too far in describing the modified Lear 75 without talking to Dr. Bern first.

"Yes, we are familiar with that particular aircraft. It was modified here in the US for Dr. Bern. Still no match for a pair of F -16's, regardless of who was flying it."

"Yes, sir. It is true, the Israeli jets did back them off, sir.

"Mr. Charles, I am calling because, frankly, we need some answers before the American Press gets them. This is very sensitive material right now. The wrong word or impression run wild could do a lot of damage."

"Yes Mr. Wilson, I understand. Matter of fact, I was just thinking of how we might be swamped up-on arrival back home. And they know where I live, and where my adult children live."

"Oh, I can tell you, Hawks and Doves alike will have their own agenda for inquiry. You won't rec-ognize what they print from what you tell them."

"I can believe that!" I said.

"Ok, Mr. Charles, here's what I would like to of-fer you, Sir. You and Mr. Bacthier, the Shah's nephew, are so hot right now that we have had to place you on the NO-FLYpLIST. Press Pomp, you know. You won't be able to fly back here commer-cially. I have been in conference with The Secretary of State and he is willing to send a military aircraft for you two to Geneva. We have flights from our Germans bases almost every day, and fly you back to Andrews Air Force base in The D.C. area. Under the express condition that we can debrief you two as to just exactly what issues you encountered."

"Mr. Wilson, that sounds like a plan to me. I am sure Mr. Bacthier will agree. We will cooperate in any way you need, sir. Then if you can drop us at Dulles, where our cars are."

"Oh yes, of course." He sounded quite pleased. "When can you come. "This is heating up quickly as it involves the Iranian nuclear build-up. Everybody is nervous about it."

"Yes sir, I understand, We are just killing a little time and getting some skiing in. Who was that blond agent that was shot by the Mossadi cab driver when she tried to kill me. I saw her back at my condo at home."

"We aren't sure, but we think she worked for German Banking interests, we are not certain as yet. You know, the German Banks do not want to have to redeem those bonds you have. They would like to decay them. They would need the serial numbers to do so. You see, we need to fill in the blanks, ourselves. There will be some military there."

"Ok.". I said.

"I will call you back with the soonest flight information."

"Ok, we can chopper back to Geneva on fairly short notice. We have a security detail that will take us to the airport there."

"Now talk to no one."

"Yes, I understand," I affirmed.

"We will talk again shortly, just need to talk to the logistics officer in Manheim."

"Yes, Mr. Wilson, we will await your instructions."

"Oh!, " Yes sir"? I want assurances that we have not committed a crime here and will need all the usual immunities."

"We see no crime here. This is a civil matter. We just want to inquire as to what the Iranians were up to," said Wilson.

"Ok, do you mind if we have our counsel present? Understand, we will give information freely but would feel better."

"Can you give me the firm's name?"

"Ah, yes," as I reached for the fax Dr. Bern had sent. "It's Catuzi & Catuzi. They have a shingle in Geneva and Palm Beach."

"I think we know of Attorney Catuzi. Good man. Fine, no problem having him present."

"Mr. Wilson, one other thing."

"Yes," he said.

"We would like new ID's if we can get them. Like in witness protection."

"I'll see what I can do, Mr. Charles. We'd like that too, less press hassle."

"Good enough, thanks."

"Bobby! Yo Bobby. Where are you?"

"Right here, man," as he emerged from his room. "What's wrong?"

"Nothing, I think I just got us a ride home safely, with our own military. We are on a no-fly-list now anyway. We have to debrief the State Department and some military. Guarantee we would have to do that anyway. Now, we will fly into Andrews

AFB, so there won't be a press frenzy. I'm thinking we could have our cars ferried or towed over there from Dulles and escape scrutiny.... Hey, Buddy, now is the time to buy a new car, anyway. Hey, I got it. Let's just buy a couple of Buicks. The're nice. And low profile. We can have them delivered to Andrews, when we get there. Buy a new tag. Don't transfer the old one." I was trying to talk and think at the same time.

"It all sounds good to me, man," Bobby was excited. "It will be good to get home. I want a red one."

"Good, I'll take straight white. Let's call Donaldson Buick on Glebe Road and line it up."

"When are we leaving?"asked Bobby.

"Soon. Waiting for Mr. Wilson at State to call back with the details. This is the best outcome. We would have gotten to the airport and run into a brick wall. I feel good about this, how about you?"

"Oh, yeah, man, let's do it, yeah." said Bobby , enthusiastically

"Let's get some sleep. I'll call Col. Reeder and Dr. Bern in the morning. And then Donaldson. If we can get the new ID's.

"Hello, Dr. Bern?" I called his private number. "We are having a great time up here. Really wonderful"

"Gut, Michael, I am glad to hear that."

"Sir, we have been put on a No Fly list! It's a tactic, a force play. Except for a private charter we would be stuck here."

"Oh, no , Michael, I will call the Catuzi attorney."

"Yes, Dr. Bern, we will need him stateside. I answered a call from our deputy secretary of state."

"Oh," he trailed off.

"We have an opportunity to fly an American Military transport out of Germany and to Andrews AFB without detection.

"We have been asked for a de-briefing session, in exchange. We, no doubt, will have to go through that anyway. Everything we have done has been above board, so we have no fear but we will want attorney Catuzi there as our guide. I am sure you may have some guidelines to employ and advise him as such. We would not want to compromise anyone.

"There is much attention back home. We want to have new Id's and we will buy new cars, not traceable to us."

"This is a gut idea, Michael."

"Would you be kind enough to give Attorney Catuzi this number for our Deputy Secretary of State, so that he might coordinate with him for our debriefing, after we arrive, stateside?"

"Yes, Give me de number, please, Michael. You always seem to have everything organized."

OK, and thanks sir, here it is. The deputy 's name is Omar Jackson and his number is 202-854-1212."

"We may need transport back to your area, too." voici

"Ok, I vill send the helicopter for you two and Colonel Reeder."

"I believe I can get us all on the transport. Reeder will feel right at home and Mr. Catuzi will save us some travel money that way and we can debrief with him first."

"Ah, yes, very Gut, Michael."

"Ok, Bobby. I've cleared with Dr. Bern. The chopper will be back here shortly. Pack up. I am thinking we can take Attorney Catuzi and Col. Reeder with us. We can brief Mr. Catuzi on the long flight over.

"We must be sure of new ID's before we bother to buy cars or there is no point. I will call Omar Wilson and be certain. Right now, we are still holding a few cards."

"Hello, Kali."

"Hi, Dad."

"Are you guys having fun?"

"Oh yeah, Dad."

"How 'bout the kids?"

"Oh, they're are great! We called Mom and she

came over too."

"Oh good" I am sure you can use the help."
"How about Jack , Cewwena and Carson."

"All good. "How are things going, over there.
Dad?"

"Good, honey. Look, I am coming home, courtesy of the US State Department, on a military transport out of Germany. It's the safest and best way to get back. They have us on a no fly list anyway. The State Department needs to debrief after that dog fight and, frankly, we need some favors too."

"When are you coming?"

"Probably start back tomorrow sometime, but you won't see me for a day or two. Just stay where you are and have fun. See all the theme parks there. I'll call you when I arrive."

"Ok, Dad. Hey, I'm gaining weight from all this junk food!"

"I can imagine." I said. "Gott'a go now"

I texted on my secure phone, **Deputy Secretary Wilson, we are ready when you are. Expect to be back in Geneva tomorrow before noon. Can be reached at my number. Charles.**

"Ok, man I think that's about it for now. We must wait to hear. Call your daughter, if you like. We should be available sometime Monday. Tell her not to mention it to anyone."

-

"Oh, no, She won't."

"We will have to wait for Omar Wilson to get back with us. Wann'a ski one time before we go?"

"Man, I don't wann'a leave this house! You don't know who might be out on those slopes!"

"Yeah, you're right. Down to the movie theater in the basement again. How about Rambo"?

"Ok. Did I ever tell you that Sly and I used to work out together when we were 14?"

"No, really?"

"Yeah, he sounded just like he does now."

We picked several Rambo's and settled down with buttered popcorn, for a long night.

The chopper was sent at 10:00 AM. In a way, I wished I had a chance to drive the distance into Geneva because the scenery was breathtaking! Stone-faced mountains with snow caps. Tall pine trees jutting up into the ski. The windy mountain roads. Could only think of what my new 'Vette would be like, driving through here.

Oh, the 'Vette!, I remembered. I would have to sell to my new name and pay sales tax all over again. $4,500 in sales tax. Well, I was so used to being poor. Better ask Attorney if there is a way around that. Now, it wouldn't amount to the interest on the interest.

We landed on the bank's Hilo Pad and went inside. Dr. Bern was gracious, as usual and introduced us to Attorney Catuzi.

"Hello Sir, we will have a long flight to brief you on the events that led up to our heist!" I said. "No, just kidding; there is nothing untoward about this transaction. Naturally, everyone wants a piece. All we're giving up is your fee!"

We all had a good laugh at at my 'Break the Ice' comment.

Dr. Bern interjected, "I spoke with Omar Wilson at the state department, this morning., He thought the military transport would arrive at Zeitweiss International at about 2:30 PM, so we have a little time yet."

Lunch had been prepared in the conference room for us all. We walked in that direction, following Dr. Bern's lead. Mr. Catuzi took a seat beside mine, with Bobby next on the right.

After a fruit cup appetizer, Attorney Catuzi just couldn't help himself and began to inquire while it was just the three of us. "Can you relate exactly what happened when you entered the bank until you left ?"

"Sure," I said. "Bobby check me out on this if I miss something or if you think it went differently."

"Ok," Bobby nodded.

"Well, we approached the bank in a cab and

while we did not know it at the time, the cab driver was a Mossad agent. I thought I detected an accent while speaking with him. Turns out we were under surveillance by various agencies for many days. We wanted to retrieve the bearer bonds and get on our way, as soon as possible.

"When we walked in, I noticed a Middle-Eastern man sitting in the lobby. He had the same insignia pin on his outer wear as I had seen on the gentleman we first met in the cave. Our contact. Also, there was a young fellow with a soccer team jersey on. He looked to be in very good shape. I just made a mental note of these two."

I related the miss-direction exercise, the run through the front door and the female agent who drew a bead on me as I left.

"That is when it was confirmed that the cab driver was, in fact, a Mossad agent himself. He shot her dead right through his open window on the passenger side."

"Did you get his name?" Catuzi said.

"No but he is acquainted with this man." I showed him Hiael's card.

"Of course, we do not want to blow their covers. Obviously, they have infiltrated the Iranians to some extent."

"I understand," said Catuzi.

"The rest was an extraction exercise. We were cleared for takeoff and were told to abort after lift off. It would have been perilous for us to try to comply with this late order. They scrambled two fighter jets, although unarmed except for a cannon. They fired a couple of volleys across, but well in front of us. They weren't going to shoot us down with the bonds on board.

"The Israeli , F18's came to our aid after we executed a maneuver and I believe our pilot hit one of the Iranian jets with our nose cannon. They bugged out when threatened with missile lock tone. They knew that by them they were out of their air space, I think.

"Once we landed in Geneva and were in transit to the bank with full security, we were attacked. I can't be certain who was behind the attack but I believe it was from the same interest who pursued us at the bank and in the airplane. I have no direct evidence of that."

The main course for lunch was being served now, so we paused while the servers were close by. It was a white fish, garnished with Snow Crab Claw and Shrimp.

"Doc, You really know how to eat around here," I said to Dr. Bern.

"Oh yes, Michael, ve have an excellent chef here at the bank."

The Chef must have been within earshot because he leaned around the corner, with a wave.

"Bravo," I said, acknowledging him".

"I am sorry to see you two leave so soon." offered Dr. Bern. "Right now, I think it's for the best to get this settled down. Please feel free to return at your earliest convenience. You are velcome anytime."

"Thank you, Dr. Bern. We will take you up on that. I love your Chalet. Thanks again for the use of it.".

"Anytime, Michael, Bobby. Bring your families for a vacation next time." He leaned over and said, "But leave the foreign agents behind next time," with a hearty laugh.

Just when we finished desert, a phone call for Dr. Bern was announced. He got up and went to his desk. "Heinz Bern here," I heard him say. "Oh yes, hello, Mr. Wilson. Yes, ETA about 30 minutes. Re-fuel and take off about three. Yes sir. Thank you, Ve vill be at ze Gate Number 6. No, thank you, Mr. Wilson. Yes sir, Col. Shank vill be their escort."

I immediately wrote down the name. so did Mr. Catuzi.

"Ok, gentleman, that was Mr. Wilson. We must be at gate no. 6 at 3:00. They are 30 minutes out but need time to re-fuel."

"Oh, good, we are ready. Heinz, thanks again for everything. We are going to miss you."

Bobby took the "Q" and did the same, with a hearty hand pump. "We will be back to visit our

money!"
A big laugh all around.

## *Deputy Secretary of State and a Free Ride Home*

We got to the Gate no. 6 and there was a huge grey aircraft with 4 jet engines hanging from its wings. I didn't know what it was but it sure was big!

Col Shank greeted us. He asked for and checked our I.D.'s and showed us to a lounge in the rear of the plane. It looked very comfortable, indeed. There was a Lt. Hopkins on hand to attend to us, make sure we were seated and buckled up. He asked if we wanted a coffee. We would be about 15 minutes yet. He indicated where a magazine rack was situated. There was a wide variety issues on hand. He handed each of us a pair of earphones, wrapped in plastic, and showed us where to plug them in.

"Wow," I exclaimed, "just like the airlines!"

"Yes sir," said Lt. Hopkins. "If there is anything you need, just ask me, sir. You all are V.I.P. status."

"Will do, and thank you, Lieutenant!

Eventually, the big plane was pushed out and lumbered down the taxiway, it's four engines winding up evermore. After 20 minutes of this, we were at the threshold of the take-off runway. I assume the pilots were getting the necessary clearances and wind and weather information.

The take off roll began. Slowly at first. *What a big beast*, I thought. We finally rotated and it was then that I realized that we had a fighter escort alongside. I looked up to Lt. Hopkins and pointed out to the escort.

"Oh yes, Sir," he said. "That's S.O.P. for these kinds of flights, Sir."

Attorney Catuzi was already reviewing his notes.

*Good*, I thought. I felt comfortable with him.

He leaned over and asked "What was the plan for the blocking of funds. The proceeds"?

"Well, now, That's why we declined. They wanted to use the proceeds to enhance their centrifuge refinement program. They wanted to spin-up some Yellow Cake, (Plutonium) But, that's not all, this gentleman, who described himself as descendent from Ancient Nehalem, he was quite tall, took us back through time, even to the Garden of Eden and elucidated a saga foreign to our ears. They were in conflict with God himself. Their plan was to place a nuclear device, suitcase size, on the Temple Mount itself, in the hope that according to sacred scripture, Christ would return to save Israel from certain annihilation. They were actually testing the hand of the Almighty. There were many quotes from scripture."

Mr. Catuzi's eyes were as large as half dollars and his mouth was open wide enough for a whole baked potato to it in!

"Well, needless to say, we got out of there. We told him we could not possibly be a part of such a thing.

"The chase came when the military got wind of our leaving with what they felt were nationalized assets. If our Lear 75 was not equipped as it was, we never would have made it so close to the limits of their space."

"How so?" Mr. Catuzi asked.

"Well we had afterburners and a nose cannon installed on that aircraft. It was modified in the US, I found out later. There has, evidently, been con-tinuous radio wave surveillance from the beginning of our endeavor. Right from Washington, DC. There were many signs in retrospect. That girl that was killed was in my condo hallways, probably my apartment before I left town. I talked to her several times. And there she was in Iran, pointing a gun at me and ready to shoot. If it weren't for that trained Mossad agent, I would be toast."

"What agent?" he said, not understanding.

"The cab driver, sir."

"Wow, this is beginning to sound like a Tom Clancy movie."

"Yes, sir." Lt. Hopkins was listening with an

obvious hyper interest, his mouth slightly open and his tongue sticking out. " Oh, sorry, sir," when he saw my glance. "I didn't mean…"

"It's ok," I shut him off with a wave of my hand. "We are all together here."

"Yes, sir," was the strident reply!

We got off the plane and there was a grey service car waiting for us. As we got in, I remembered my gun in its high leg mount. Government building? No thanks. I reached under and proffered it un loaded to the officer up front. "I have a license to carry this, sir, but we are going to the holy place." I laughed and offered my Glock to him.

"Understood," he said.

Attorney Catuzi also offered his Glock over. "I almost forgot. Wow! What a mess that could have been."

A group of terrorists-like individuals, five in all, moves into Dr. Bern's' bank

Dr. Bern is upstairs in his office. A Teller is taken. hostage in the hope that security cameras will see it from the control center. They know there are security cameras in upstairs offices, viewing the lobby.

Three go to the private elevator after an employee held at gun point shows them where it is.

Before anyone notices and forces a 'lock down.' they burst through the office door. Automatic weapons are discharged into the ceiling.

Dr. Bern scrambles, thinking this is a simple robbery. But everyone upstairs is rounded up and brought to the dining room.

A security guard runs into the room at the sound of gunfire. They take his firearm.

Terrorist immediately ask that a security monitor be brought to them so they can extort from the hostage downstairs. Picture is shown of teller downstairs, held hostage.

"You are Dr. Bern, I presume?" Revealing a middle eastern accent.

"Yes, vhat do you want?"

After hearing the accent , Dr. Bern was getting a clue as to what was going on. The bonds, naturally, he considered, since he had received threatening phone calls a short time ago.

"We want those German Gold Backed Bearer Bonds that belong to the people of Iran."

"I do not think so, sir," said Bern, "and they are locked in the vault. Open by timer only."

"Then Mrs. Downstairs, will have to die!"

"You vill never get out of here anyway," said Dr. Bern. An old combat Colonel, he had no fear. "The building is, by now, on lockdown and a silent alarm has been sent out to the authorities."

"Those bonds belong to the people of Iran!"

The invaders protested.

"No they don't! After this invasion, who will liquidate them for you anyway? No collector vill touch them."

"Sirens could be heard approaching outside.

"We must have those bonds." they reasserted.

"I cannot give them to you!" said Bern. "The serial numbers have been recorded and they will be decayed by the Bundus Bank. Ve heard vhat you were planning to do with the proceeds." Dr. Bern was Jewish and was getting plenty mad now at that thought. As noted, he had been through WWII, himself!

Six rounds of a neutralizing gas were fired through the front door window and rear door before anyone could act. Gun fire was directed at the high ceiling of the bank. Two shock Grenades were detonated, by the S.W. A. T. team.

There were screams but in a few seconds everyone was asleep on the lobby floor, harmless.

While this distraction was going on, another security guard upstairs ran into the room, and drew his revolver. The terrorists with the assault rifle let loose a another burst but the security guard was deadly accurate first and hit him through the head once.

Then he panned his weapon until the others froze. "Who's next?" he yelled like a madman, leaving no doubt that he wanted to shoot someone else.

Dr. Bern got on P.A. system and told the police, now fully positioned swat team, "We are all secured. Captain, please come up elevator to Executive suite. He assumed there was a captain present.

As we were escorted into Department of State Office and the inner sanctum, Omar Wilson introduced himself. There was a long table and at least ten people present. Water pitchers and glasses for all. Also a legal pad for notes

"We are entering DC and I need to give the Glock into your custody."

"Oh yeah," said attorney Catuzi, "me too," as he presented his gun. Short hours later, we were on approach to Andrews AFB but we had fallen asleep.

Omar gives a cast of characters, introducing us to these men around the table. They include some very serious looking gentlemen from 1) Mossad 2)The NSA 3) The CIA and 4) The FBI for stateside issues.

We were surprised at the scope of the cast .

"Gentlemen, I am sorry to begin with bad news. The bank in Geneva has been attacked by terrorists. This afternoon! They wanted the bonds in question, claiming they belong to the Iranian people."

I gasped stood up and screamed at the top of my lungs, "Nooooo!:

Bobby stood up and declared. "They are my inherited property. They have been in that box for nearly 70 years."

"Ok, I have had enough crap from these people! How is Dr. Bern?" I asked.

"As far as we know at this time he is ok." 're-turned the DSS as he extended both hands in a motion to calm down. "We are requesting the immediate presence of the Iranian ambassador as we speak."

Attacking that good old man was off the charts. They didn't want to see this street scrapper get motivated. This was a mission!

I turned to the gentlemen identified as Mossad and said, "You have to stop these guys! They are committed to placing a nuke on the Temple Mount. Maybe in their own Dome of the Rock. They will sacrifice it. They still have the Hag. They are blind idealists who agenda is other-worldly! I think they will strike you. Get prepared! Whatever the US or any other allay says!

"It will destroy Israel in seconds. Sure there will be retaliation but Israel will be gone by then. If your leaders have an attack plan in place, now is the time to strike first. This is sinister. A Jihad."

The DSS was on his feet, urging calm. "I better call the Secretary of State in to hear this" and he left the room for a minute, presumably to retrieve his boss in person.

Before the Secretary of State arrived, I added further, "Listen, if you're waiting for our President to act in concert with you, consider this. I am a civilian but right now a pretty rich one. So, consider this. Our President is not engaged because he reacts to crises . He is not pro-active. He has never run anything in his life. He really hasn't even had a decent job before. He was an organizer of nominal voters for the former ACORN which was as crooked as a pretzel. Don't blame him that he is in way over his head. His election was an exercise in penance. He has no depth in these things. We are governed through a kid in a toy store! We have no right to expect Statesmanship from him. Think about it. And forget the P.C.

"He is having a ball with his airplane, golf clubs and movie stars. He was little more than a drug addict, by his own admission, before then. His wife was about to leave him.

"He was groomed by one Mr. Resco for the Illinois Legislature for special interests issues and voted present most of the time. You can't get his school records and one wonders how he even matriculated at Harvard. Classmates in the same curriculum don't even remember seeing him.

"Actually, with the costs involved, he almost had to matriculate as a foreign exchange student. His birth certificate is a work of art! Bad art! This guy has played us like a Stradivarius. He pinches himself every day. Yes, Yes, we are hedonistic fools. But we are talking about the welfare of your country. Otherwise, you'll read about your fate on a teleprompter. In a split second it could be reduced to rubble.

"These rogue people want to force and confrontation with the Christian God! They think He will come back and intervene, perhaps setting them free.

"If there were a way to neutralize their refining machines or their raw material without a hit it, would have been done already. They really don't care if they put us all back to the stone age. They've already been there!

"Bam, Bam, I call him, because he's such a kid sometimes, ain't goanna act first and that's what you need here! Forget the impotent UN ! Too many politics. Once you have Bam, Bam firmly by the right balls, Not the golf balls, his mind will soon follow. He will have to. You better Launch. I, personally am going back to the Swiss Alps and find a cave!"

A Mossad member said, I must call the General about our contingency plans. And the Ambassador," he quickly added.

CIA, NSA and FBI couldn't deny the cogency of this diatribe. They were scrambling out of the room! They could see there was no turning back now.

As they were making a door jamming exit, (Looked like Larry, Moe and Curly) the Secretary of State walked in with his deputy. "Ah, what, what is going on here! Did we miss something?" as each spun around with their hands splayed submissively apart, bumping shoulders with those exiting. The SS had such beautiful hair! He instinctively reached up to hand groom it, a nervous compensatory habit from his youth.

We sat back down like the Cheshire Cat.

"What happened here?" the Secretary of State demanded. And looked menacingly at the four of us. Col. Reeder and Attorney remained with us.

"COOL HAND LUKE," I said.

"What? What do you mean, Cool Hand Luke? What kind of an answer is that? The SS was red faced.

"WHAT WE HAVE HERE IS A FAILURE TO COMMUNICATE."

EPILOG

It was simple, after all. A small EMP devise was detonated high above the center of Iran. Chaos ensued just long enough for the 1st wing, division to target and strike the area with deep penetrating bunker bombs. There were over a hundred. Just before the EMP was launched but before munitions were rained down, a radio announcement was disseminated in all pertinent languages via a 100,000 watt transmitter giving 15 minutes to evacuate their facilities of all personnel. Iranians would not be able to launce in such a short time. The attack and neutralization of the threat was completely successful.

P.O.T.U.S. called to say, "Hello, I was just getting ready to suggest..... @$%^&)*, Damn teleprompter! Was the last thing the Israelis heard.

Meet our author
Michael Plunkett

Born in 1946, second in a family of six children, in the then sleepy Southern town of Washington, D.C., where secretaries wore white gloves and hats when going to lunch. This, just before the migration of workers from the south expanded government offices. Michael's father's business would take him as a helper into many government buildings, agencies and international Embassy's where, as a curious adolescent, he would glean all he could from the desks of Ed Murrow, U.S.I.A. Radio Free Europe propaganda, many embassy's and the private homes of George Will, Walter Lipmann, Ray Chalk and others. This early exposure to the workings of government led him to Liberal Arts and the study of Political Science at Montgomery College in Rockville, Maryland and on to a Pre-Law curriculum.

Psychology and religious studies became hobbies with copious reading in both disciplines. Descendent from the Rommel's on his mother's side—Irwin, the Desert Fox, and Bishop Oliver, now Saint, on his father's side, there were conflicted spirits in his closet.

Ever the adventurous one whether flying planes or riding super motorcycles at excessive speeds, he had to have the hair on fire and ride in the wind to feel at home.

In his books he incorporates his adventures and knowledge of people through thousands of intimate interviews in his business career where he had become a National sales director and executive vice-president of a prominent marketing company with tens of millions of dollars in sales productions each year. This is where he met the Shah's nephew and many other unique characters.